"We cou
who you are, why you are—"

Quinn's mouth came down on hers, cutting Hayley off. Then, as if every nerve in her body had been jolted into awareness, heat flooded her. For an instant it seemed as if he were as stunned as she at the sudden conflagration. But then he moved, encircling her with his arms, pressing her against him as he deepened the kiss.

Hayley's every nerve was sizzling. She couldn't feel her knees anymore, and her arms felt heavy, weak. But it didn't matter, none of it mattered, not as long as Quinn was there, holding her— she wouldn't fall, he wouldn't let her. All that mattered was his mouth, coaxing, probing, tasting.

It was going through her in pulses now, that surging, delicious heat, like nothing she'd ever known. Some tiny part of her brain tried to insist it was because it had been so long, but Hayley knew it wasn't that, knew it had never been like this in her life, because she'd never kissed a man like Quinn before....

★ ★ ★

Dear Reader,

Ever have a dog that was too smart for its own good? One that could open doors, cupboards, or con that last treat—or bit of your own dinner—out of you? One that could make you laugh at the drop of a hat, or comfort you when no one and nothing else could? Wait, that pretty much describes all dogs in one way or another, doesn't it?

But let me tell you about Cutter. He's a composite, I suppose, not just of my own dogs over the years, but others I've met. From the one who could pick just my horse out of the herd, to the one helping his mom to weed by carrying the offending plants to the wheelbarrow, to the one who delighted in rides on an office chair, to the one who knew with her first glimpse of my ill husband who she was here to rescue. (That is the real meaning of "rescue dog," you know.)

It's not really that big a stretch from there to a dog who is not just very, very smart, perceptive and brave, but—well, I'll just have to let you see for yourself. I hope you enjoy this first story, about two people who didn't know how much they needed each other. Who didn't even know each other yet. Humans are so slow sometimes that a dog just has to take charge....

Happy reading!

Justine

JUSTINE DAVIS

Operation Midnight

ROMANTIC
SUSPENSE

Recycling programs
for this product may
not exist in your area.

ISBN-13: 978-0-373-27765-0

OPERATION MIDNIGHT

www.Harlequin.com

Printed in U.S.A.

Books by Justine Davis

Harlequin Romantic Suspense

Always a Hero #1651
Enemy Waters #1659
‡*Operation Midnight* #1695

Silhouette Romantic Suspense

Hunter's Way #371
Loose Ends #391
Stevie's Chase #402
Suspicion's Gate #423
Cool Under Fire #444
Race Against Time #474
To Hold an Eagle #497
Target of Opportunity #506
One Last Chance #517
Wicked Secrets #555
Left at the Altar #596
Out of the Dark #638
The Morning Side of Dawn #674
†*Lover Under Cover* #698
†*Leader of the Pack* #728
†*A Man to Trust* #805
†*Gage Butler's Reckoning* #841
†*Badge of Honor* #871
†*Clay Yeager's Redemption* #926
The Return of Luke McGuire #1036
Just Another Day in Paradise #1141
The Prince's Wedding #1190
One of These Nights #1201
In His Sights #1318
Second-Chance Hero #1351
Dark Reunion #1452
Deadly Temptation #1493
Her Best Friend's Husband #1525
Backstreet Hero #1539

Baby's Watch #1544
His Personal Mission #1573
The Best Revenge #1597
Redstone Ever After #1619
Deadly Valentine #1645
  "Her Un-Valentine"

Silhouette Desire

Angel for Hire #680
Upon the Storm #712
Found Father #772
Private Reasons #833
Errant Angel #924
A Whole Lot of Love #1281
Midnight Seduction #1557

Silhouette Bombshell

Proof #2
Flashback #86

Silhouette Books

Silhouette Summer Sizzlers 1994
  "The Raider"

Fortune's Children
The Wrangler's Bride

†Trinity Street West
*Redstone, Incorporated
‡Cutter's Code

Other titles by this author available
in ebook format.

JUSTINE DAVIS

lives on Puget Sound in Washington. Her interests outside of writing are sailing, doing needlework, horseback riding and driving her restored 1967 Corvette roadster—top down, of course.

Justine says that years ago, during her career in law enforcement, a young man she worked with encouraged her to try for a promotion to a position that was at the time occupied only by men. "I succeeded, became wrapped up in my new job, and that man moved away, never, I thought, to be heard from again. Ten years later he appeared out of the woods of Washington State, saying he'd never forgotten me and would I please marry him. With that history, how could I write anything but romance?"

For Nikki, the first, when I was too young to understand.

For Whisper, who taught me so much, and deserved better than I and life gave her at the end.

For Murphy, because without him there might not have been a Decoy (and now his sister Bailey, too).

And for Chase, who proves that boys can be sweet, too.

To all the sweet, funny, smart, wonderful dogs I've known. But most of all for The Decoy Dawg who, against all odds and predictions, at this moment has seen another summer. I love you, my sweet girl. I won't give up until you do. And when you do, I'll try to let go with the grace you've taught me.

Chapter One

"Cutter!"

Hayley Cole shouted once more, then decided to save her breath for running. It wasn't that the dog was ignoring her. Sometimes he just got so intent on something, the rest of the world ceased to exist.

Serves you right, she told herself, *for spoiling him. Treating him like a human just because half the time he acts like one.*

That he'd shown up on her doorstep when she most needed him, that she now couldn't imagine life without the uncannily clever Cutter didn't help at the moment, as she was traipsing after him through midnight-dark trees. If she hadn't known these woods from childhood she might be nervous, but it was the wrong time of year for bears, and she wasn't afraid of much else. But a sassy dog could get into trouble; just last night she'd heard coyotes. And a cornered raccoon could be nasty. While she had faith in the clever dog's ability to come out on top, she didn't want him hurt in the process.

At least out here, if you heard a sound in the night, your worry wasn't who, but what. Well, maybe except for that blessed helicopter that had buzzed the house a while ago, setting Cutter into the frenzy that started this whole chase. They weren't uncommon in the Pacific Northwest, what with the navy and coast guard coming and going. Normally they didn't ruffle the dog, but this smaller one had been frighteningly low and had set him off like a rocket.

She dodged around the big cedar tree on the north side of the trail that could barely be found in full daylight. She should have grabbed her heavy, hooded parka with the flashlight in the pocket, but while fall was in the air it was still merely cool at night, not cold. Besides, she hadn't realized this was going to be a lengthy expedition.

She was on her neighbor's property now, and she doubted the reclusive older man would welcome either her or her four-legged mischief maker, so she forged onward.

"Like some stupid character in a bad horror movie," she muttered under her breath, rethinking sharing the last of the beef stew she'd made with the carrot-loving dog.

She rounded a large maple and nearly tripped over Cutter, who had stopped dead.

"Whoa," she said, recovering. "What—?"

The dog's tail gave an acknowledging wag, but his attention never wavered. He was staring through the trees at something. A little wary—it *was* too early for bears, wasn't it?—she moved up beside the dog to look. For a moment it didn't register, it seemed so unlikely.

In the darkness it was almost indistinguishable, in fact would be invisible if not for the faint light from the house. That light slipped over polished, gleaming black, so that the shape she saw was a series of faint reflections, curved and straight, rather than the object itself.

But she still knew what it was, instantly.

The helicopter that had rattled her windows fifteen minutes ago was sitting in her reclusive neighbor's yard.

Something about the thing sitting there, glimmering faintly in the dark, unsettled her. The fact that it had no apparent markings unsettled her even more. Weren't they like planes? Didn't they have to have numbers on them?

Maybe it's a prototype, her logical mind said. Hasn't been registered yet. Lots of aircraft industry up here in the Pacific Northwest. Maybe her neighbor was a designer or something. She had no idea what he really did, nor did any of the others in this semirural, forested little community. Being mostly kind, they didn't call him antisocial, at least not yet. The speculation ranged from eccentric hoarder to grief-stricken widower, depending on the mind-set of the speculator. Hayley, who herself valued her privacy and the quiet of this wooded setting, preferred to simply leave him alone if that's what he chose.

Being right next door, she'd seen him more often than anyone, which meant exactly twice. And both times he'd retreated immediately inside, as if he feared she might actually approach him.

But now she was wondering if a little more curiosity might have been wise. Scenarios from mad scientist to terrorists foreign and domestic raced through her mind. Her mother would have laughed at the very idea of such things in quiet little Redwood Cove, but her mother had been unaware of many dark things in the world in the last years of her life. Not by choice, but because she was focused on the battle to extend that life as long as possible, a battle Hayley had fought beside her for three years, until it was lost eight months ago.

She heard a sliding door opening, and in the next instant a bright light on the side of the house came on. Instinctively she jerked back, even though the apparently motion-sensing floodlight didn't reach this far. Cutter, on the other hand, took a half step forward as two men stepped out onto the deck. His nose lifted, twitching rapidly as he drew in the scents the faint breeze wafted his way.

The light threw the helicopter back into the realm of, if not ordinary, at least no longer sinister—at least it did until she realized she could now see that indeed, there wasn't a single marking to identify the craft.

The light also made the silver in her neighbor's neatly

trimmed beard gleam. The second man, much younger, with a buzz cut and a leather jacket, was a total stranger. He seemed to be helping the older man as they went down the steps, gripping his arm in support.

Her breath caught as, coming down the steps into the yard where the helicopter waited, the leather jacket parted and she saw a holstered handgun on his hip.

She grabbed Cutter's collar; all her silly notions about men in black and their black helicopters suddenly didn't seem so silly anymore. Were they the good guys, if any still existed, and was her neighbor being arrested? Was the reason for his reclusiveness something worse than she'd ever imagined?

She shivered, wishing more than ever for her parka. And then another thought followed rapidly: What if he was the good guy? What if these men in the black helicopter were the bad guys, and her neighbor was being snatched by them? That it could be some twisted combination of both also occurred to her; these days it was harder than ever to tell bad guys from good.

The two men got into the helicopter, the younger one again helping the older, with every evidence of solicitousness. Moments later, the helicopter came alive, engine humming, running lights blinking on.

Her mind was racing. Two men, one of them armed, get on the helicopter, and it starts up. So obviously, unless her neighbor was the pilot, which seemed unlikely, the other man was. Which had to mean her neighbor was going willingly, didn't it? Otherwise, wouldn't he run while the other man was occupied with...well, whatever you did to fire up a helicopter? Unless he couldn't. Perhaps he wasn't well enough? Or was simply too frightened to try to escape?

Or...could there have been a third man, waiting aboard the craft all this time?

Cutter made an odd, uncharacteristic, whining sort of sound just as a movement on the deck caught her eye. And she realized there was at least a third man, because he was coming out of the house now. Tall, lean, with hair as dark as the sky.

He had a large duffel bag slung over his left shoulder. He started down the deck steps, and two things happened simultaneously. The sound of the engine got louder. And Cutter let out a sudden, sharp bark.

Before she could react, the dog had twisted free of her loose grip on his collar. And to her dismay he bolted, straight toward the third man. Tail up, head down, he raced out of the trees and across the open yard. Cutter was never vicious, but the man he was charging didn't know that, and she took off after him.

So much for a silent retreat, she thought as the man, obviously having heard the dog's bark, dropped the duffel bag to the ground.

"Cutter!"

The dog ignored her, intent on his target. But he was running happily, joyously, as he did when he greeted her if she'd been away and left him home. Some part of her mind wondered if perhaps he knew the man. She'd never seen him before; now that he'd turned in their direction she knew she wasn't likely to forget a guy who looked like this one.

She had a split second to wonder if the mystery of Cutter's appearance in her life, at the time when she'd needed the distraction most, was about to be solved.

The man turned to face the dog's onslaught.

And pulled a gun. Aimed it at Cutter.

"No!"

Panic lifted her shout to a scream. He didn't shoot. It should have been reassuring. Except that he instantly turned his attention—and his weapon—on her. She kept going. He hadn't shot Cutter, and he had to be a lot more threatening than she was.

Then again, maybe not, she thought, her pace slowing as the dog reached his goal. And while she'd never expected him to launch into an attack, she certainly hadn't expected what he did next; the dog sat politely at the man's feet, then looked over a furry shoulder at her with an expression of utter delight. His tongue lolled happily, his ears were up and alert and he looked just as he did when he found the exact toy he'd been searching for.

He looked, for all the world, as if he were saying, "Look, I found him!"

The man lowered the lethal-looking black handgun but did not, she noticed, put it away.

She grabbed Cutter's collar, firmly this time.

"I'm sorry. He got away from me, but he's harmless, really. He doesn't usually... I mean, he's usually a bit slow to warm up to strangers. He doesn't generally charge up to them..."

She was babbling, she realized, and made herself stop.

"I'm sorry," she repeated. "We didn't mean to trespass." She glanced at the waiting helicopter, gave an embarrassed smile, hoping her neighbor could read her expression since he doubtless couldn't hear her inside and over the noise of the engine.

"Damn."

Her gaze shot back to the man who had just muttered the curse. The light was behind him, silhouetting his rangy frame, making him seem even taller, looming over her. Her gut told her the quicker she got them out of here, the better. She tugged on Cutter's collar, but the dog was reluctant and reacted with uncharacteristic resistance.

Everything the darn dog had done since that helicopter had buzzed the house had been uncharacteristic, she thought, tugging again.

The door of the helicopter opened. The first armed man she'd seen leaned out.

"Time, Quinn," he shouted over the noise of the engine and the growing wind of the main rotor.

"I know."

Hayley heard the exchange and registered that the man her suddenly recalcitrant dog seemed so attracted to was apparently named Quinn, but she was mainly focused on getting them both out of here. Normally she was able, barely, to lift Cutter if she had to. But dragging him when he was actively resisting was something else.

She turned, intending to walk away, hoping the dog would

just follow; normally he always did, not liking her too far away from him. Not that he was behaving normally just now, but—

She gasped as the man called Quinn suddenly appeared in front of her, blocking her path. She hadn't even heard him move. And in that instant the entire scenario went from ominous and unsettling to threatening. Because clearly this man was not going to let her just walk away.

"I'm sorry," the man said.

Then he grabbed her, so swiftly she had no time to react. He ran his hands over her, so obviously searching that any thought that it was some personal assault never really formed.

She elbowed him. "What do you think you're doing?"

It was a rhetorical question, and it got the answer it probably deserved: nothing. She tried to pull away again but he held her in place with ease, warning her without a word that he was much stronger than she.

And then he lifted her off the ground. She fought, clawing, kicking, landing at least one solid blow. She barely had time to scream before she was physically tossed aboard the helicopter. She twisted, trying to get out before the man called Quinn got aboard. Cutter, she noticed through her panic, did nothing but whine in obvious concern. Somehow she'd always assumed the dog would defend her, would attack, bite—

She was pushed down into a seat. She scrambled to get to her feet, but Quinn leaned over and grabbed Cutter, tossing the fifty-pound dog into her lap as if he weighed no more than the duffel bag that followed. And then he was aboard himself, and the door slammed shut behind him with grim finality.

She sat in the seat he'd shoved her into, her heart hammering, her hands shaking as she clung to Cutter, fighting to wrap her mind around one simple fact.

They were being kidnapped.

Chapter Two

"You were no help at all," Hayley muttered to the dog overwhelming her lap. Yet despite her surprise at that—a tiny emotion next to the fear that was growing every second—she clung to the furry bundle. The dog didn't seemed bothered at all by what was happening, just as he hadn't protested by even a yelp when this total stranger had grabbed him, never mind her.

She, on the other hand, was terrified. If she hadn't had the dog to hang on to, to focus on, she was sure she'd be shrieking. And then the rotors began to turn, and she did let out a little gasp.

"Thanks for the help, Teague," Quinn snapped at the other armed man. Even though he was practically yelling to be heard over the engine and growing rotor noise, the sarcasm came through.

The other man laughed. And grinned, a boyish, crooked grin she would have found charming under other circumstances. Now it just added to her growing fears.

"The day you can't handle a woman and a dog is the day I quit this gig," the man called Teague shouted back.

"I let you fly, so get us out of here."

Teague's grin flashed again, but then he was all business, turning his attention completely to controls that, Hayley noted, seemed to take not only his hands and eyes, but feet, as well. Flying a helicopter was apparently a complicated affair.

"Belt up," Quinn instructed her.

Hayley didn't react, still watching the pilot as she tried to analyze the easy, friendly banter between the two men. Did that bode well, or worse? She didn't know, and—

"Let go of the damn dog and put your seat belt on." He was yelling again now as the sound of the engine and rotors increased again.

There was too much dog to just let go of and get her hands on the belt she could see at her sides. And then the man realized that, grabbed Cutter and again lifted him as easily as if the animal didn't weigh almost half what she did. To her annoyance, the dog didn't even growl at the usually unwanted liberty taken by a stranger. But she kept her mouth shut. She didn't want to anger the man while he had the dog in his arms.

He seemed to realize that. "You want him back, do it."

She reached for the belt ends, then glanced back at her traitorous dog. Just in time to see him swipe a pink tongue over the set jaw of their captor.

"Talk about fraternizing with the enemy," she muttered as she fastened the harness-style belt, figuring she was safe enough saying it aloud, it was so noisy in here.

The only saving grace was the expression on Quinn's face; utterly startled. She wasn't sure how she knew it was not an expression he wore often, but she did. He plopped the dog back into her lap.

"Must you?"

The barely audible question came out of the darkness beside her, and Hayley realized it had come from her neighbor, the first time she'd ever heard him speak. His voice was a bit raspy, probably, she thought wryly, from disuse. And she thought it might hold a bit of an accent, although it was hard to tell from two words called out over the noise of a helicopter.

"Sorry, Vicente," Quinn said, sparking another spurt of annoyance in her; if anybody should get an apology, it should be her, shouldn't it?

Teague yelled something Hayley couldn't hear well enough to understand, but Quinn must have, because he turned his head to answer. Then he reached out and picked something up from the empty front seat. If she had any guts, now would have been a chance, while he was turned away. She could lunge for the door, get away. Problem was, she didn't think she could undo the belt, hang on to Cutter and get the door open fast enough. She—

Quinn turned back, and the moment was lost. To her surprise, he jammed himself onto the floor at her feet, although he was tall enough to make it a tight fit. It took her a moment to realize he was staying to keep an eye on them, rather than strapping himself into the vacant seat beside the pilot. That must have been, she thought, what that exchange she hadn't heard was about. And what he'd picked up was some kind of headset, perhaps something that enabled him to talk to the pilot, or at least muffled the noise that made normal conversation impossible.

And then she felt the undeniable shift as they went airborne into the midnight sky, and it was too late to do anything but try not to shiver under the force of the sheer terror that was rocketing around inside her. Why on earth had he done this? She'd done nothing, had been more than willing to vanish back into the woods and let them go. All she'd wanted was her dog....

She clung to her furry companion, his thick, soft coat warming her hands. If there were lights inside this thing they weren't on, but she didn't need them to visualize the dog's striking coloring, the near-black face, head and shoulders, fading to a rich, reddish brown from there back. The vet said he looked like a purebred Belgian breed, but since—despite being the smartest dog anyone she knew had ever seen—he hadn't shown up with papers, she didn't know for sure.

And as comforting as the dog's presence was—even if he did seem inordinately fond of their kidnapper—she regretted it now. The dog was indeed clever, sometimes to the point of seeming unnaturally so. More than once since the day he'd appeared and proceeded to fill the void in her life, she had wondered if he was really just a dog. He seemed to sense, to understand, to *know* things that no ordinary dog did or could. And because of that, he would be safer on the ground, able to survive on his own. At least for a while.

She didn't want to think about the possibility that it might be longer than a while. Much longer. That it might be forever, if these men had lethal intent.

She hugged the dog so tightly that he squirmed a little. What had her bundle of energy and fur gotten them into? The dog didn't seem at all bothered by the fact that he was airborne. He seemed to be treating it as if it were merely a more exciting version of the car rides he so loved.

She ducked her head, pressing her cheek to Cutter's fur. In the process she stole a glance sideways, to where her neighbor was seated, carefully strapped in. She still couldn't see much of him, just the gleam of the silver-gray beard, and a faint reflection from his eyes. He'd said nothing else through this, in fact after his query had seemed to shrink back against the side of the noisy craft, as if he were wishing he could vanish as he had on the two occasions she'd come across him outside his house. She wondered what he was thinking about her sudden intrusion into his affairs, inadvertent though it was.

But at least he'd made a token protest. She supposed that counted for something.

Vicente. She'd never known his name. And from the way he'd asked the question, hesitantly, it seemed clear he wasn't in charge of this operation, whatever it was. Was he rich, was that what this was all about? A kidnapping for ransom? But if so, why was he so cooperative? Not that guns didn't engender cooperation, but he'd seemed awfully willing.

Besides, why would somebody who could afford an aircraft like this one need money so badly they'd commit a crime like kidnapping? Unless of course that was *how* they afforded it.

Maybe they were drug dealers, she thought, barely resisting the urge to look around and see if there were drugs piled in the small space behind her. Did helicopters have separate cargo spaces? She had no idea. She pushed the media-inspired image of wrapped white packages of cocaine out of her mind.

There were other possibilities, of course. Terrorists, for instance. They didn't look it, but what did she know? Maybe Vicente was some sort of master bomb maker, maybe they—

The helicopter seemed to lean sharply, cutting off her careening thoughts. *Just as well,* she told herself, *you were getting silly.*

At least, she hoped she was getting silly. But what simple explanation could there be for being scooped up in the middle of the night by strange men, along with her possibly stranger neighbor?

She lifted her head, realized Quinn was staring at her from his spot on the floor. She had no idea what he might be hearing in that headset, but there was no doubt about what he was looking at. As with Vicente, all she could see was the reflection of what dim lights there were in his eyes, and a different sort of gleam on the dark, thick hair.

Since talking and asking the myriad of questions she had was impossible, her mind was free to race to turn over every rock looking for possibilities. This was not necessarily a good thing, she realized. She'd never thought of herself as particularly imaginative, but the things that tumbled through her mind now could be called nothing less. In the light of day, anyway.

Quinn seemed focused on her, as if he wasn't worried about Vicente at all. And if that were true, that confirmed her neighbor was part of this, in some way. It made her shiver anew to think what the man might have been up to just a couple of hundred yards away from her home. That he might have had very good reason to stay hidden.

Cutter returned the scrutiny, keeping his eyes on the man on the floor, occasionally stretching out toward him with his nose, apparently still in love at first scent. It really was strange, the way the dog had reacted to this man. Under other, normal circumstances, she might be inclined to trust the dog's judgment; more than once he'd been wary of someone she'd later learned was worthy of the distrust. And if he liked someone... well, at the moment the jury was out on that.

And it finally occurred to her to wonder why the man had brought the dog along. He'd only hesitated a fraction of a second before picking him up and putting him in the helicopter after her. Had he assessed that quickly that she'd do what she had to to protect the animal? Including cooperate with him?

The more she thought about that, the more it frightened her. That he had realized, that quickly, that Cutter could be the key to her cooperation told her more than she wanted to know. Clearly whoever and whatever he was, he would use any tool that presented itself.

She stared back at the man, her mind providing an image of what she couldn't see in the darkness, filling in details she'd glimpsed in the deck light. The strong jaw, the stern mouth, the dark brows with the slightly satanic arch—

Okay, that's enough of that, she ordered herself, and looked away. At least his image would be clear enough to tell someone what he looked like, she thought.

Someone? Like the police?

Her breath jammed up in her throat, unable to get past the sudden tightness as the obvious belatedly hit her. She'd seen them. All of them. But why hadn't they just killed her on the spot, then? Had they been in too much of a hurry to get away? Or had they just not decided her fate yet?

More likely, she thought grimly, they had a place where they disposed of bodies, and it was easier to wait until they got there.

And all her imaginings suddenly didn't measure up to the horror of the reality, and even the darkness couldn't make it any worse.

They flew on and on, until her half-crazed mind would have

sworn it had been days if it weren't for the fact that they were still and ever in darkness.

And underlying it all was the grimmest imagining of all, that she might never see the light of day again.

Chapter Three

"Coming up on the airport in about ten."

Teague Johnson's voice came through loud and clear over the headset, with none of the crackle or hiss the old headsets had been prone to. Worth the price, Quinn Foxworth thought as he lifted the flap on his watch that kept the dial's glow from being seen. 0315 hours. Not bad, well within the parameters they'd set despite the...complications.

"Fuel?" he asked.

Normally it wouldn't be an issue, they planned carefully, but they were carrying an extra passenger. And a half, he added with a grimace. That dog....

"It made a difference," Teague answered. "It'll be close, but we'll make it."

"Copy."

He went back to his study of their unplanned-for passenger, while that half-passenger continued to study him. The dog's dark eyes never left him, and he didn't have to be able to see in the dark to know it, although his night vision was remarkably good.

He knew little about the workings of the canine brain. And had no idea why the dog seemed so…taken with him. It would be amusing if it wasn't so puzzling.

His owner, on the other hand, wasn't taken with him at all, Quinn noted wryly. Too bad. She wasn't bad-looking. At least, from what he'd seen. And felt, during his cursory pat down and when he'd put a hand on a curved, tight backside to shove her aboard. It had startled him, that sudden shock of interest; there'd been little time for women in his life for…a very long time.

And there was no time now, he told himself. They'd be on the ground soon, and vulnerable for the few minutes it would take to refuel. And it had better be only a few minutes; they'd paid enough extra to guarantee it. They could have avoided this by using a plane, with longer range, but in this semirural area it would have meant transporting Vicente by ground to an airstrip, and then from an airstrip to the location on the other end. And that would have made them even more vulnerable.

The unexpected intrusion of woman and dog hadn't delayed them much, since he hadn't wasted any time dithering about what to do. But it was costing them more fuel; even though she looked to weigh maybe one-twenty at most, the dog added another forty-five or fifty pounds—five of that fur, he thought—and together that was the equivalent of another passenger about Vicente's size. On an aircraft this small it mattered, not so much in space as in fuel efficiency. But their timetable, and getting Vicente out of there, had been the most important thing.

And secrecy. The man was a valuable commodity, and they couldn't risk leaving behind somebody who could tell anyone anything.

He felt the shift in angle of the chopper, knew they were approaching the small airfield where they would refuel. He saw the woman's head come up a moment later, as she apparently realized it, too. Her gaze shifted to the port window, then, obviously able to see nothing but night sky, shifted forward, as if she were trying to read the controls for a clue.

Could she? Did she know something about helicopters, or aircraft gauges? She didn't seem to be affected by the flight, no sign of air sickness or dizziness when they had made any quick changes. Unlike Vicente, who had required a serious dose of motion sickness medication to tolerate the flight. Quinn had been glad to give it to him; drowsiness was a side effect, and that was fine with him.

He'd thought about making the woman take some, too, under the guise of not wanting her to throw up in his helicopter. But there hadn't been time, and getting it down her would have been too much hassle. Besides, he wanted a chance to assess her under controlled circumstances. And there weren't many more controlled circumstances than strapped into a helicopter seat at ten thousand feet and a hundred and thirty-five knots.

So far, she hadn't been trouble, but he wasn't about to turn his back on a woman who rushed a man with a drawn weapon. And even when her face had been hidden as she clung to that damned dog, he couldn't escape the feeling that she was thinking like mad, and that didn't bode well for keeping things simple.

As they dropped lower she became more alert. He smothered a sigh; as if he could hear her thoughts, he knew she was trying to figure out a way to escape. He reached out and slid down the built-in shade on the porthole she'd been looking out; the more ignorant they could keep her of the surroundings, the better.

He flicked a glance at Vicente, who seemed to be sound asleep, propped in his corner. He was a tough old bird, he'd give him that. He'd barely turned a hair when they'd shown up in the middle of the night and taken over. But given his history, that wasn't surprising.

But this young bird, this wary, watchful female of the species, he didn't know. So he had to assume the worst.

"It's all yours when we touch down," he said into the headset.

"Problem?"

"The old man's asleep. Our uninvited guest is plotting."

"What'd she say?"

"Nothing. And how do you know I didn't mean the dog?"

He heard the short laugh. "The dog clearly thinks you're some kind of dog-god. The woman, not so much."

"Figures," Quinn muttered.

Another laugh, and as if in punctuation they dropped rather sharply.

"Got the signal light," Teague said.

Moments later he set the craft down with the gentlest of thumps, barely perceptible, nearly as soft as he himself could have managed. He'd have to let the guy fly more often, Quinn thought.

The noise lessened as the rotors slowed. The fuel truck was already there and waiting, as planned, a good sign. He would have preferred to keep her running, but the crew here wasn't trained for a hot refuel so they had to shut down. They didn't want the kind of attention flouting the local rules would bring. The anonymity of the small field was worth it, they'd decided.

Teague waited until the rotors had stopped, then opened his door and stepped down to the tarmac. There was a floodlight on the side of the hangar they were closest to, and it brightened the interior of the helicopter. Quinn glanced at Vicente, making sure he was truly sleeping; he hadn't seemed to stir at all, even when they'd landed. The old man better not be getting sick on them. But his eyes were closed and Quinn could hear, in the new silence, the soft sound of snoring. Maybe the guy just was particularly susceptible to those meds, he thought.

The quiet seemed deafening, nothing but the brief exchange between Teague and the fueler and the sounds of the process audible in this dead time between night and morning. He'd read somewhere that more people in hospitals died at 3:00 a.m. than any other time, that it just seemed to be the time people gave up.

Not sure why that had occurred to him just now, he wondered if he could just leave the headphones on and stave off

whatever she had in mind. But the moment it was quiet enough
to be heard, she dove in.

"I need a bathroom."

Ah. So there it was, her first approach, he thought. Short,
to the point, grounded in reality, and hard to deny. But deny
he would; they couldn't risk it. For what it told him about her,
he filed it away in his mind in the section he'd labeled "uninvited guest."

"Hold it," he said, brusquely, taking the headphones off.
He stood up, even though he had to hunch over; he needed to
stretch his legs after the hours of being cramped on the floor.

"I can't."

He nodded toward the dog. "If he can, you can."

She drew back slightly. When she spoke, her tone was that
of teacher on the edge of her patience to an unwilling-to-learn
child. "He's a dog, in case you hadn't noticed."

Definitely got a mouth on her, Quinn thought.

"I noticed," he said drily. And now that he could see her
better, could see that his earlier impression had fallen short of
the reality, he silently added, *and I noticed you certainly are
not.*

He felt another inner jolt, a flash of heat and interest, more
intense than the first time, fired further by thoughts of that
mouth. He clamped down on it harder, angry at himself; he
never let anything interfere on a job. It was why jobs kept
coming.

"Then you should know he can hold it longer. How do you
think they wait all night inside a house?"

"I never thought about it," he said, although now that she'd
said it, it sparked his curiosity. "Why can they?"

She seemed startled by the question. But she answered rea-
sonably. "My guess is it's because when they were wild, they
had to, to hide from predators. Now will you please find me a
bathroom?"

"Hold it," he repeated.

"I'm a human, not a wild animal," she snapped.

"You think humans weren't wild once?"

"Some," she said pointedly, "still are."

He ignored the jab. "So hold it," he said a third time, trusting his instincts and her body language that this was just a ruse to get out of the helicopter and onto the ground, where she likely figured she could make a run for it. Not a bad plan, and just about the only one possible given her circumstances.

"Humans haven't needed that talent since we hit the top of the food chain," she said.

Oh, yeah, a mouth. And a quick wit. If he wasn't otherwise occupied, he'd like to find out just what else went on in that mind of hers.

And he interrupted his own thoughts before they could slide back to that mouth.

Teague was back then, announcing they were all fueled up. As he started to climb back into the pilot's seat, the woman turned her plea on him. The younger man looked startled, then disconcerted, and Quinn had to admire the way she switched to the younger, possibly more vulnerable target.

"Bathroom?" Teague echoed. He flicked a glance at Quinn. "She can wait."

"How would you know?" There was the faintest change in her voice. Her snappishness had an undertone now, just a slight flicker. But he recognized it; he'd heard it too often not to.

Fear.

Now that he thought about it, it was somewhat amazing that it hadn't been there before. Something he should remember, he told himself. *She doesn't scare easy, or she hides it very well.*

"You'll wait."

"Want a mess in your pretty helicopter if we're in the air when I can't?"

"Then I'll push you out." She drew back, eyes widening. He pressed the point. "Or maybe the dog."

She gasped, as if that thought horrified her even more. *And there's my lever,* he thought, as her reaction confirmed what he had suspected from the moment he'd seen her racing across that stretch of open yard after the animal. She'd risk herself, but not the dog. She'd protect him, no matter what.

He pounded the point home.

"He won't save as much gas as you would, but maybe some."

She stared at him, saying nothing, but he could almost hear her mind racing, trying to analyze and assess if he really meant what he'd just said.

"Get us out of here, Teague," he said, and reached for the headphones. He put them on before they were really necessary, and pretended not to hear her call him an epithet he'd last heard from the lips of his ex-wife. Except she'd said it sadly, ruefully, whereas there was nothing but venom in this woman's low, husky voice.

Still fighting, he thought, but not stupidly. She didn't try anything she was doomed to lose, like getting past him, or striking at him.

He filed the knowledge away in his head as he settled into his cramped spot on the floor, shifting once to avoid pressure on the spot on his left leg where she had kicked him. She'd fought hard. He was lucky she hadn't gotten his knee—or worse—with that blow, or he'd be gimping around for two or three days. As it was, he was going to be feeling it for at least that long.

And if looks could kill, he'd already be dead.

Chapter Four

This wasn't the first time Hayley wished she had a better sense of direction. Without the little compass reading in her car's rearview mirror, she'd never know which way she was going, unless she was headed into a rising or setting sun.

She wasn't sure a good sense on the ground would translate to a good one in the air, however. And while she was sure this beast must have a compass, it was situated where she couldn't see it from back here, so she had no idea which way they were headed. They'd changed direction more than once, and she was completely lost now.

Her sense of time passing was pretty good, though, and she guessed they'd been airborne this second time over a couple of hours. Almost as long as the first leg, which she had pegged at around three hours. So they were better than five hours away from Vicente's front yard, and her own little house among the trees. A long time in cramped quarters; even Quinn had shifted so he could stretch out his long legs on the floor of the craft.

I hope your butt's numb by now, she thought uncharitably. *Even if it is a very nice one.*

She quashed the traitorous thought; not every bad guy was a troll, after all. The world would be in much better shape if they were, of course, but life was never that simple. If they were the good guys, surely they would have pulled out a badge and shown it to her by now, to ensure her cooperation?

She tried to puzzle out at least how far they'd come, but she had no idea how fast they were flying, and without that crucial factor of the equation, what she did know was useless.

The only thing she knew for sure was that her dog was about at the end of his considerable patience. He'd begun to squirm again about a half hour after they'd taken off the second time, clearly wanting down off her lap. Since it was awkward, overheating and by this time generally uncomfortable to hold the animal, who seemed to get heavier with every passing moment, she'd looked for a space to let him down. But there was little, not with Quinn on the floor in front of her.

It occurred to her she should just dump the adoring Cutter in the man's lap. That perhaps she should have done that while they were on the ground, then maybe she could have gotten to the door while he disentangled himself.

But that had never really been an option. The man still had a gun, and he'd already threatened to pitch the dog overboard. That had been when they'd still been on the ground, but she wouldn't put it past the steely-eyed man to do it when they were airborne.

Cutter squirmed again. He gave it extra effort this time, and it worked; his hind end slipped off her knees and she couldn't stop him. He gave a final twist and she had to let go or risk hurting him. And in the next moment, he was exactly where she'd thought of pitching him; in Quinn's lap.

Her heart leaped into her throat. Her common sense told her the man wasn't likely to shoot inside his own helicopter, but she was scared and this was her beloved pet, and logic wasn't her strongest point just now.

"Please, he's just a dog," she said urgently, leaning forward as far as she could belted into her seat, hoping he would hear her over the noise of the flight.

He said something, but so quietly she knew it was meant for the pilot. She held her breath, praying it wasn't an order to open the door so he could toss the animal to his death.

They kept flying. Quinn lifted the fifty-pound dog easily off his lap. And then, to her amazement, he bent his knees and turned slightly, wedging himself into what had to be a much less comfortable position, and put the dog down on the floor beside him.

He'd moved to make room for Cutter.

Hayley closed her eyes, nearly shaking with relief. She didn't know what to think, now. It was such a simple thing, but yet so telling.

Maybe.

Maybe he just didn't want to risk opening the door and tossing the dog out. Or the mess of shooting him. She fought to hang on to the cynical view, knowing it was both the more likely, and safer for her to believe, for Cutter's sake and her own.

Gradually she became aware that she could see a little better. She cautiously looked around, wondering if Quinn would try to stop her from doing even that. From where she was, thanks to the shade he'd pulled down, she could only look forward. It seemed the sky looked lighter along the horizon there, but without the rest of the sky to compare it with, it was hard to be sure. Quinn, down on the floor with Cutter, who was apparently happy now, was still in darkness. But the fact that she could now see Vicente's face where he'd been in stark shadow before told her her guess about time was accurate. Dawn was breaking.

She saw Quinn's head move as he put a hand to the headphones as if listening. She guessed he spoke then to the pilot, or perhaps answered something the pilot had said.

If they'd been headed east there was geography to deal with, and that little problem of the Cascade Mountains. Could a helicopter even go high enough to get over them? Or would it have to fly along the same passes and routes used by men on the ground? She had no idea.

You really don't know much useful, do you? she thought sourly.

But who would have ever thought she'd need to know how high or fast a scary black helicopter could fly? Just the phrase *black helicopter* was so laden with images and ideas from books and film that it made clear thinking almost impossible.

Vicente moved slightly, shifted position. For a moment she wished she'd been able to sleep as well as he seemed to have; her weariness just made rational thought even harder. But sleeping under the circumstances, especially with the lethal Quinn—for she had no doubt he could be just that—barely a foot away, was beyond her, even tired as she was. Fear-induced adrenaline was still coursing through her system, and she was jittery with it.

Vicente moved again, then opened his eyes. With the added light, she was able to see him go from sleepiness to awareness to full wakefulness, and he sat up sharply. And when he looked her way, a parade of expressions crossed his face, first surprise, then recognition as he remembered, and then, somewhat mollifying, regret.

It was at that moment she realized they were dropping in altitude. Another refueling stop? Well, this time asking for the bathroom wasn't going to be a ruse, it was going to be a necessity. And if he didn't believe her this time—

The sharp pivot of the helicopter interrupted her thought. They were definitely landing. This time she recognized the feeling. And as the direction they were facing changed, she saw indeed the first light of dawn on the horizon.

They touched down even more lightly than last time, so lightly she wasn't sure they were actually down until Teague began to flip off switches and the sound of the rotors changed as they began to slow.

And then, as she got her first glimpse of their surroundings in the still-gray light of dawn, she wondered if they were here to refuel at all. Because this certainly was no airfield, not even a small, rural one. And there was no sign of a fuel truck.

What there was, was a big, old, ramshackle barn several yards away across an expanse of dirt dotted with low, scraggly-looking brush. A bit beyond that was what appeared to be an old, falling-down windmill. And coming toward them from the barn was a man, dressed in khaki tan pants and a matching shirt that made him hard to see against the tan of the landscape in the faint light. Hayley thought he might be limping, just slightly, but she couldn't be sure. What she was sure of was the rifle he held. Not a classic, elegant one with a polished wood stock, but an all-black, aggressive thing that looked as if it was out of some alien-invasion movie.

Quinn pulled off the headset, and this time instead of putting it in the empty front seat, hung it on a hook overhead. Did that mean they were here? Wherever "here" was? Was this their destination?

Quinn pulled himself to his feet, dodging the now-alert-and-on-his-paws Cutter. He looked at Vicente, who was now sitting upright, fully awake.

"We'll have you inside shortly, sir," Quinn said.

Sir?

Respect, she noted. While she obviously didn't even rate an acknowledgment, now that they were...wherever they were.

"I really need that bathroom now," she said.

Quinn glanced at her. Seemed to study her for a moment. She didn't know what he saw that was different, but he apparently believed her this time.

"It'll only be a few minutes." Then his glance shifted to the dog. "He can get out now, though."

Hayley didn't quite know how to take that; was it thoughtfulness for the dog, or did Quinn want control of him, so that he could control her?

If that's his thinking, he's in for a surprise, Hayley thought. About the first part, anyway; she didn't think anybody really controlled Cutter.

Quinn got out of the chopper, and she saw him bend and

stretch his legs as if they were cramped. They must be, cramming a body she guessed was at least six feet tall into that small space on the floor couldn't have been easy. Not that she felt sorry for him.

But he had made room for Cutter, despite the cramped quarters. And the dog seemed no less enamored of him this morning than he had been from the moment he'd encountered this dark stranger.

But to his credit, he did hesitate when Quinn held the door open for him. He looked back over his shoulder, his dark eyes fastened on her in a silent appeal for permission. She selfishly wanted to tell him no, wanted him to stay with her, but she knew the sometimes-hyperactive dog was probably about to jump out of his fur after being trapped in this small space for so long. Not to mention he probably needed his much more convenient sort of a bathroom as much as she needed one.

"Go ahead," she told him, and with a small, happy woof, he leaped from the helicopter to the ground. He looked up at Quinn expectantly. Quinn seemed puzzled, and made a broad gesture toward the open space they were in, as if to tell the dog it was all his now. It was strange how much smaller Cutter looked standing next to the tall man; to her he seemed like a big dog, next to Quinn, more average.

Cutter briefly checked out the surprised newcomer, but despite the aggressive weapon, and unlike with Quinn, after a moment he seemed to find nothing of particular interest there and quickly moved on at a brisk trot, checking out his new surroundings.

The new man was speaking to Quinn and Teague, in the manner of someone giving a report. Teague was listening carefully, but it was clear the report was directed at Quinn. To Hayley, everything sounded a bit muffled; her ears must be humming a little after the hours of noise, and she could make out only an occasional word; she heard the newcomer say "perimeter" and "secure," but not much else.

"I am very sorry."

Her head snapped around as her fellow passenger spoke

into the fresh silence. He did have a slight accent, Hispanic, she thought, and he was looking at her with that same expression she had seen earlier, tinged with more than a little regret.

That she had gotten sucked into this? she wondered.

Or that she wasn't going to get out of it?

At the moment, the latter seemed more likely. And by the time Quinn turned back and gestured her out, she was oddly reluctant; the stealthy black helicopter seemed suddenly safer than whatever she was going to be stepping into out there.

Chapter Five

"We're up and running," Liam Burnett said briskly as he joined sniper Rafer Crawford in reporting in.

Quinn nodded as he stretched gratefully; he'd expected nothing less. His crew was well trained and could think for themselves. They'd have everything ready to roll.

Then Liam spotted their extra half-passenger roaming about, and Quinn could see his detail-oriented mind kick in. And then he noticed the woman still aboard, and that mind revved up even further. Quinn followed the progression of his thoughts as they went from the logistics of an extra person and an animal, to the realization that person was a woman, to the recognition that she was a rather attractive one. Liam always had had the worst poker face of them all. Came with youth, Quinn supposed.

"So," Rafer said, with a sideways glance of his own at the woman still in the chopper, "how'd *she* happen?"

"Unavoidable," Quinn said with a grimace, and gestured with a thumb toward the dog, who was ranging out toward the barn, investigating the grounds with a thoroughness he had to admire. The animal would probably know who and what had been through here for the past six months before he was through.

"The dog's fault?" Rafer sounded even more puzzled.

"It's a long story," Quinn said as he watched Teague open the far door of the helicopter and help Vicente out. The older man moved stiffly, almost gingerly. Rafer quickly went to help; he had some experience with moving through pain.

"We have any painkillers in stock?" Quinn asked Liam. "Seems the old man's got arthritis pretty bad."

"Standard first-aid kit issue, plus Rafer's stash of ibuprofen."

"May have to raid that," Quinn said. "Hope he's not having a bad week."

"Seems okay," Liam said.

Since Liam and Rafer worked together a lot, he should know, Quinn thought. As much as anyone did, anyway; Rafer did a good job of hiding any pain the old injury gave him. If it wasn't for the slight limp, no one who hadn't seen the impressive scar would know there was anything wrong. And he refused to let it slow him down; it had been a long, painful process, but he'd pushed so hard and learned to compensate so well he was as efficient as any of them at anything short of long-distance running.

"Sometime today?"

The words came from inside the helicopter. She was sounding a bit snappish, Quinn thought, smothering a wry quirk of his mouth.

"If you're lucky," he retorted, not even looking at her.

"What's her name?" Liam asked, lowering his voice.

"No idea."

Liam stared at him for a moment, then shook his head ruefully. "Only you could spend all this time with a woman who looks like that and not even find out her name."

"If you're so interested, you watch her," Quinn said drily. "You might find her more trouble than she's worth."

"I don't know," Liam said, giving her a sideways look, "she looks like she'd be worth a lot."

"I'll get her inside while you secure and refuel the chopper, then she's all yours," Quinn said. He reached over and yanked open the door. "Keep her under control."

From the corner of his eye he saw the woman stiffen, drawing up straight. She'd reacted to his last words much as he'd expected, and he felt a tug of relief as he handed responsibility for her over to the young and earnest Liam. If she was the girl-next-door type her loyalty to the dog suggested, they'd be perfect for each other.

"What about the dog?" Liam asked, keeping his eyes on the woman as she emerged from the helicopter.

"Our other uninvited guest? I'll round him up," Quinn said. "He seems to like me."

"No accounting for taste," the woman muttered, and he saw Liam smother a grin.

"No, there surely isn't," Liam said, no trace of the grin on his face sounding in his faint Texas drawl.

Quinn watched as she stepped down to the ground. It was past dawn now, and he could see what he'd missed before. She was a little taller than he'd first thought, maybe five-five. The curves were definite but not exaggerated. And the hair he'd thought was simply brown in fact was a combination of brown and gold and red that made the chill morning air seem warmer.

I think you've been cooped up too long, he told himself, smothering another grimace.

"She says she needs a bathroom," he said, quickly reducing things back to the basics. He thought he saw her cheeks flush slightly as he announced her needs to all present, but as he'd guessed, it truly was a necessity this time, because she didn't protest.

But then she turned and got her first look at where they were. And her thoughts were clear on her face; he had the feeling that, maybe for the first time in her life she really, truly knew what the phrase "the middle of nowhere" meant.

They were on a slight rise, but as far as the eye could see around them was nothing but empty, nearly flat land, unrelieved by anything but dried-up grasses, scrubby plants and an occasional tree. It wasn't desert, at least not the kind the word summoned up in his mind—sand and wind and dunes—but it was very, very far from the green paradise they had left last night.

He could almost see her hopes of escape plummet; not that he would have let her get away anyway, but she wouldn't be the woman he was beginning to think she was if she hadn't at least been thinking about it. But he saw the realization of the odds that she would make it to any kind of help or even civilization dawn in her eyes as she looked out over the remote emptiness.

"Be careful what you wish for," she said softly, in an almost despairing whisper.

It didn't take a genius to guess what she meant; all those hours when she'd probably been wishing the interminable helicopter flight would end, and now that it had she wanted nothing more than to get back on the thing and get out of here. Because that seemed the only way to leave this utterly isolated place.

Good, Quinn thought. As long as she realized that, hopefully she wouldn't try anything stupid.

And then she turned around, and saw the cabin.

She really did have an expressive face, Quinn thought. Playing poker with her would be like taking money from a baby, even more than Liam. Not that he really blamed her. The cabin looked as if it was about to fall in on itself. All but a strategically placed couple of windows were boarded over, and the roof sagged and looked as if it would leak like a sieve, if it ever rained in this place. There were loose pieces of siding here and there, and things at odd angles and heavily weathered. The only solid-looking piece of it was the river-rock chimney, standing as a testament to the skill of the long-ago stonemason. The place looked as if it had been abandoned for years.

It looked exactly as it was supposed to look.

"Quinn?"

He turned to look at Liam. "The dog. Are we going to need a run into—"

The words broke off as Quinn gave a warning flick of a glance at the woman. Admittedly the nearest little town, tiny though it was, was not one she'd likely heard of, but he didn't want to give her any ideas.

"Don't worry about feeding the damned dog."

The woman went still. "He has to eat," she said.

Quinn didn't even look at her.

"I'll get everybody inside, and out of sight," he told Liam. "You get with Teague and secure the bird."

Liam nodded.

"He has to eat," she said again.

He turned then. "Shouldn't you be worried about how and whether we're going to feed *you?*"

She never hesitated. "He comes first."

He blinked. "He's a dog."

"I'm responsible for him. He trusts me to take care of him. It's part of the deal."

He thought she might be getting a bit esoteric about it, but he couldn't deny he admired her sense of responsibility. And thankfully, Charlie believed in overkill when it came to stocking up for an indefinite stay.

"He can eat what we eat, for now."

She seemed to relax a little at that, letting out a breath of relief. And she still didn't ask if that *we* included her. He watched the dog for a moment as he sniffed around the barn. And then, as if aware of Quinn's gaze, the dog turned, head up, looking toward them. And unbidden, started toward them at a tail-up trot. He really was a distinctive-looking dog, with alert, upright ears and a dark head and thick ruff that gradually shaded back into a lighter, reddish-brown coat over his body. He looked intense, like the herding dogs he'd seen in Scotland on the many pilgrimages he'd made.

"His name's Cutter?" he asked, almost absently as he

watched the animal cross the yard between the ramshackle barn and the even more ramshackle cabin.

"Yes," she said. "And mine is Hayley, not that you bothered to ask."

No, he hadn't asked. Hadn't wanted to know. Had been much happier when she'd just been "the woman," an unexpected annoyance that had to be dealt with.

"Don't tell me," he said. "Tell Liam. He thinks you're a welcome addition to the scenery."

Like you don't? a traitorous little voice in his head spoke up.

But she didn't seem bothered by the implied aspersion. Instead she looked around at the barren landscape before saying with a grimace, "Middle of nowhere, careful what you wish for, and now damning with faint praise. My life's suddenly full of clichés."

Quinn nearly gaped at her for a moment as her first words echoed his exact thoughts of earlier. Any other normal woman he could think of would be in hysterics by now. Or at least too frightened to think straight, let alone come back at him with wit. He was beginning to think she was going to be more than just a fuel-eating inconvenience.

He'd better tell Liam to keep a *really* close eye on her.

Chapter Six

Hayley stopped dead in the cabin doorway, startled. No, beyond startled, she was stunned. After the outside, she'd been expecting thick dust, holes in the walls, broken furniture if any and traces of wildlife.

Instead, she was confronted by a spotless and amazingly whole and modern interior. Most of the main floor was one big room, the upper level an open loft that looked down into the main room. There was new-looking furniture that was surprisingly nice. A sofa in a soft green and tan, and four armchairs in a matching green, seemed to echo the colors outside. Yet where they were drab out there, inside they seemed soothing. There were loose pillows on the sofa for lounging, and a knitted green throw for cozying up in front of a fire in the big stone fireplace. Decidedly—and unexpectedly—homey. Except for the large, utilitarian metal locker that sat between the door and one of the few unblocked windows.

There were even coordinating area rugs on the floor, which was wood burnished to a high sheen, although it was slightly uneven and looked distressed enough to be the original. It fit, she thought. With the big, square coffee table, it was a comfortable and inviting setting. Which shocked her to no end.

"I thought you wanted a bathroom."

Quinn's voice came from right behind her, sounding clearly impatient.

"Judging from the outside, I didn't expect one inside," she snapped.

To her surprise, his mouth quirked at one corner, as if he were about to smile. If so, he efficiently and almost instantly killed the urge.

She stepped inside, looking around even more intently. There was a big table with eight chairs, in the same style as the coffee table, over near a half wall that formed what appeared to be the kitchen. There was a compact stove, a small refrigerator, and even a microwave sat on the counter, so clearly they had power. Which, come to think of it, was puzzling as well, since she hadn't seen any power lines. Not surprising; if they told her they were literally a thousand miles from nowhere, she'd believe it. A generator? She hadn't seen that, either, or heard it. They weren't uncommon where she lived, she had one herself, and she'd never heard a truly quiet one.

Maybe they're environmental fanatics and there are solar panels hidden somewhere, or maybe that windmill wasn't really broken and had been converted to power production instead of pumping water, she thought, not finding the idea particularly comforting. Zealots of any kind made her nervous.

She nearly laughed at herself. Nervous? How about terrified? Spirited off in the middle of the night by one of those black helicopters that had become a cultural myth....

Something else registered as she studied the kitchen area. Instead of cupboards there were open shelves, and they were clearly well stocked with easily stored food, some canned, some freeze-dried, some packaged. So well stocked, her stomach sank; just how long did they plan on keeping them here?

"In there," Quinn said, pointing toward one end of the room where a narrow hall led off to the right.

The need was rapidly approaching urgent, so she followed

his gesture. For a moment she wondered if he was going to follow, to watch, and she frowned inwardly. But, in one of those constant trade-offs of life, dignity lost out to bodily imperative.

To her relief, he let her shut the door. Probably, she thought as she flipped on the light and glanced around, because there was no window in the small bathroom. The sink, with a narrow cabinet, was in the far corner, with the toilet—thankfully—opposite. There was no tub, and the stall shower was tight quarters; she couldn't imagine a man the size of Quinn using it easily.

Oh, good, she thought caustically, *let's start thinking about the man in the shower, naked and wet.*

Although she had to admit, it would be a good way to keep her mind off the fact that he'd kidnapped her and dragged her off to a place that looked, on the outside at least, as if it could belong to some crazed, manifesto-writing bomber or something. Probably about the only thing that could keep her mind off it; for all he'd done, she couldn't deny Quinn—was that his first or last name?—was a fine-looking man.

"The laws of the universe really should include one requiring bad guys to look like trolls," she muttered as she finished making use of the facility.

Then she turned on the water, quickly washed her hands and dried them on the hand towel politely waiting on a wall hanger. With the outgo problem resolved, she took a quick drink, her dry mouth and throat welcoming the soothing wetness. Then she left the water running while she investigated the cabinet and the small medicine chest.

She found nothing but more towels, and unopened packages of soap, toothpaste, toothbrushes and safety razors. She pocketed one of those, even as she told herself they were called safety razors because you couldn't do any major damage with them. It just made her feel better, and she left it at that.

And then, for the first time, she looked in the mirror over the sink. Bleary, tired eyes stared back at her. And as if they'd been a signal her brain had until now been too revved up to hear, a wave of weariness swept her.

She shouldn't be so tired, she told herself. She'd often pulled all-nighters with her mother in those last, grim days. She'd learned then to nap in small increments when she could, getting just enough sleep to keep going. And that had gone on for months, so one sleepless night, even a stressful one, shouldn't make her feel like this.

Maybe being kidnapped is a different kind of stress, she thought, then nearly laughed aloud at herself, trying to be reasonable and logical when her entire world had gone insane.

"The water supply isn't endless."

The sharp words came from outside, and with a start she quickly shut the water off. When she opened the door, Quinn was leaning against the doorjamb, left thumb hooked in the front pocket of his jeans, his right hand loose at his side. Keeping the gun hand free? she wondered, scenes from a dozen movies coming to mind. Did he really think she was going to attack him or something?

It was all she could do not to reach into her jacket pocket and finger the razor she'd snagged.

"Find anything?"

The question was pointed, in the tone of a man who knew perfectly well there was nothing to find, and was just letting her know he knew she'd looked.

"I'm sure you already know the answer to that. What do you think I'm going to do, sharpen a toothbrush?"

"No, although it's been done. You might want to use one, though."

She instinctively drew back; was he saying her breath needed it?

He's just trying to keep you off balance, she told herself. And succeeding, she amended sourly.

"How kind of you to offer," she said sweetly. "Should I waste the water?"

His mouth quirked again, but he only shrugged. "Just don't

be profligate. You're already an extra person. Unless you want the dog to go thirsty."

"He's going to need water," she protested instantly. "In case you hadn't noticed, he's got a pretty heavy coat."

"Not my problem."

"Yes, it is. He didn't ask to be dragged off to the middle of this desert, wherever it is."

"Then you can give him your share."

She would, of course, if it came to that. "I didn't ask for this, either," she reminded him.

For the first time she saw a trace of weariness around his eyes. Blue eyes, she saw now, in the growing morning light. Very blue.

"I know," he said, that barest hint of weariness echoing in his voice. "But there was no choice."

Was he softening, just slightly? She was torn between wanting to demand answers and a gut-level instinct that she might be better off not knowing the answers.

"I am very sorry, miss."

The quiet words came from her left, and snapped her head around. It was her neighbor, looking at her with troubled dark eyes.

"It is my fault," he began, formally, still apologetically. "I—"

"Enough, Vicente," Quinn cut him off sharply. "Don't talk to her."

Hayley smothered a gasp, as if he'd slapped her. So much for any softening, she thought angrily. Vicente sighed, and retreated to the living room. Then Quinn turned on her.

"You, get upstairs. And stay there. Don't leave except for the bathroom."

She had to fight the urge to scamper up the narrow stairs like a skittish cat. It took every bit of nerve she had to meet his gaze.

"He was just trying to apologize."

"And he did. Go."

"Cutter—"

"We'll round him up later, if he hasn't taken off."

Her mouth quirked this time, at the very idea of the loyal animal deserting her. Even if he was fascinated by their captor.

"Never had a dog, have you?" she asked.

His brow furrowed, as if thinking her words a complete non sequitur. Then, slowly, a distant sort of look crept over his face.

"Not in a very long time," he said, not even looking at her. And Hayley couldn't help wondering what inward image he was seeing.

It lasted only a couple of seconds. Then the cool, commanding Quinn was back. And even she could tell he was out of patience, such as it was.

"You going, or do I have to drag you?"

"Going," she muttered.

Liam was coming in as they came out of the hallway.

"All set," he said. "You guys came in on fumes."

"Extra weight," Quinn said.

Hayley kept her expression even this time; he'd gotten to her with the toothbrush comment, and she wasn't going to let it happen again.

"Not much," Liam said, eying her with male appreciation that was a marked contrast to Quinn's sharp impatience.

"She goes up in the loft. And don't forget the dog," Quinn said with a grimace.

"Who could be very handy," Liam said, shifting his gaze to Quinn. "Warned Rafer off a rattlesnake out there."

Rattlesnake. Wonderful, Hayley thought. Her home was blessedly free of the venomous types, so this was a new one. She had no problem with a nice garter snake, or the helpful kings, but—

"Don't like snakes?" Quinn asked.

Did the man never miss anything? "I'm talking to you, aren't I?" she snapped.

Liam let out a whoop of laughter. Quinn gave him a sour look.

"She's definitely all yours," he muttered, and walked away.

Chapter Seven

Quinn wasn't one to believe in omens or premonitions, but as he stood in the doorway of the cabin, he was starting to have a bad feeling about this. Usually one or two, or even more, little things would go wrong on a job. Didn't mean a thing. And this job had gone like clockwork—until they were leaving the target's location.

Then, from the moment that damned dog had blasted out of the woods at him, things had gone to hell.

The dog. Where was he, anyway?

On the thought, the animal trotted around the far end of the barn where, if there were more delays and this turned into a long stay, the helicopter would be stored. With the ease of long discipline he managed not to think of the ramifications of a long stay with a recalcitrant, smart-mouthed woman, one he just knew wasn't going to settle into any easy waiting routine.

The dog's head and tail came up, and he started toward Quinn at a gallop. Quinn shook his head in puzzlement. Why would a dog he didn't even know act like this? He'd never even seen such a dog, with that distinctive coloring. He was a very square, lean animal who moved with a swift grace that Quinn could appreciate.

Teague had apparently been following the dog, and as he came around the barn he gave Quinn the hand signal that meant hold. Quinn had put the order out for silent ops, until they knew they hadn't been seen or followed. And thankfully, he thought as he watched the dog slow to a trot, then came to a halt in front of him, the dog didn't seem to be a barker.

Quinn waited, guessing from the signal Teague had something to report. Almost absently, he reached down and scratched the dog's ears. The blissful sigh the animal let out made one corner of his mouth twitch, and it was all he could do to keep from smiling. He didn't get it, this sudden and inexplicable reaction from a strange dog, but he had to admit it was...enjoyable. Flattering. Something.

Teague slowed to a trot, then a halt, much as the dog had. The man's right arm moved, then stopped, an oddly jerky motion. Teague was the newest member of the squad, and Quinn guessed the movement, if completed, would have been a salute. It would be a while before he got over the automatic response.

"Go," he said with a nod.

"Yes, sir. Perimeter's clear. But he—" he gestured at the dog "—found some big animal tracks in the gully on the north side."

"Animal tracks?"

"Just a couple. I might have missed them, they were up under the lip, only reason they weren't erased by the wind, I guess."

So, as Liam had said, the dog could end up being useful. Quinn's brow furrowed as he remembered some of the K-9 teams he'd worked with in the past, and he filed away the idea of adding one to the crew.

"Any idea what?" he asked.

"They were blurred, but paws. Big ones. Don't have wolves out here, do they, sir?"

"More likely a mountain lion."

The man blinked. Although well trained and fearless, Quinn knew Teague was a born-and-bred city boy. He knew what he needed to know for survival in the wild, but it wasn't second nature to him as it was with many on the various crews.

He'd come to them through their website, where his long, thoughtful, articulate posts had first drawn the attention of Tyler Hewitt, the webmaster, who sent them to Charlie, who in turn had started sending them to Quinn. Unlike many, Teague had survived the incredibly long and difficult vetting process without faltering, and the first time Quinn had met the young former marine in person, he'd known he'd be a good fit.

That had been just before the flood, the deluge of dissatisfaction that had swept the Corps and the other branches. They could, if they wanted, pick and choose now, from a multitude of skilled, experienced warriors who had had enough, had finally realized just what was happening. Quinn didn't want any of them.

He and Charlie had picked a date, somewhat arbitrarily, but a date that became the marker; aware before that and they still had a shot. Not, and…not. He wanted men like Teague, who had been smart enough, aware enough, and had the brainpower to see the patterns and read the proverbial handwriting on the wall. And see it early, not just when it became so obvious that the lowliest grunt couldn't miss it.

And no one above a certain rank, he'd added. Once you got that high, there was no way you couldn't see what was happening unless you purposely ignored it. It cut them off from a lot of experience, but to Quinn the other was more important.

"Tracks seemed old," Teague was saying. "And he—" again he gestured at the dog "—was very interested but not…frantic."

He ended the sentence hesitantly, as if he wasn't sure the word conveyed what he meant, but Quinn got the image immediately. He nodded in approval.

"Then you're likely right. They're old. But tell the others, we'll keep an eye out just in case."

"And I'm guessing the dog will let us know if it comes back," Teague said.

Quinn looked down at the patient animal at his feet. "Probably," he agreed, "but we can't rely on it. He's not trained and we don't know him well enough."

"You know, it was funny, out there. It almost seemed like…"

Teague trailed off, looking a bit awkward.

"Like what?" Quinn asked, reminding the man with his quiet tone that in this world, his opinion was welcomed, and sometimes even acted upon.

"Like he *was* trained. I mean, I've only worked with K-9s a couple of times, but it was like that, the way he seemed to know why we were out there, the way he tracked, searched almost in a grid."

Quinn's gaze shifted back to the dog, who sat patiently still, looking up at him with a steady gaze. As if waiting for further orders. Was it possible? Did the animal have some training? He looked too young to be a retired police or military dog, and moved too well to have been retired due to injury. Was he a washout of a program, for some other reason? Or was he just darn smart?

The thoughts about the dog brought him back to thinking about the dog's owner. And that brought on the need to move, to do something, anything.

"Good work," he said briskly. "We're in two-man teams. Four hours on. You and Rafer take first watch. Work out who does what between you, but I want that perimeter checked every quarter hour. Liam and I will relieve you at—" he glanced at his watch, the big chronograph that told him more than he needed on this mission "—eleven hundred hours."

"Yes, sir!" Again Teague barely stopped the salute. Quinn gave him a wry smile.

"It takes a while," he told him.

"It's not just that." Teague hesitated, then plunged ahead. "It's being able to salute a boss who deserves it."

And that, Quinn thought sourly, was what happened when

you assigned a young, honest, decent, smart kid to work for brass who thought only of their next political move and made every decision based on how it might move their personal agenda forward. If Teague had been in a combat unit, he would have lasted a lot longer.

And he wouldn't be here, which would be their loss, Quinn thought.

"Thank you." He acknowledged the tribute with more than a little sadness. "Now get to it."

The young former marine turned on his heel smartly and headed out to connect with Rafer, who had just emerged from the barn where he'd been checking on the big power generator. He saw Quinn, gave him the "Okay" signal; Rafer was the mechanical guy on the team, and if he said the generator was okay, they were set for as long as the fuel lasted. The big underground tank held enough to keep them going for a month, if they were a little careful. If this turned out to go longer than that, then refueling would become an issue.

If this turns out to go longer than that, insanity is going to become an issue, Quinn thought. They really were out in the middle of a lot of nowhere.

Middle of nowhere, careful what you wish for, and now damning with faint praise. My life's suddenly full of clichés.

The woman's words—he refused to think of her by name, it would be better if she remained just the woman, the glitch, the impediment, the nuisance—rang in his head. Oh, yes, she definitely had a mouth on her. And the wit and spirit to use it.

And both were things he'd be better off not thinking about.

Chapter Eight

Hayley drew back from the banister that topped the three-foot-high wall running along the edge of the loft. Her anger had ebbed slightly now, allowing her to think. Her father had once told her that anger fogged the brain, and she'd never had a clearer demonstration than just now.

It was absurd, after all, to have anger be the thing her brain seized on when Quinn had told her neighbor not to speak to her, as if she were some sort of pariah. Absurd indeed. But anger, her father had added, was still better than despair. At least it was more useful, if channeled properly.

She sat in the single chair in the long but narrow space, realizing she needed clear thinking now more than she ever had in her life. While her mother was ill, she'd gotten used to having to fight through the cloud of exhaustion for every decision, for the steps of every action, had been aware she had to be extra careful simply because of it, careful not to make a mistake she would normally never make if she weren't so tired.

She was tired after the harrowing night without sleep, but

that was nothing compared with months on end of sleeping less than four hours at a time. She could do one sleepless night standing on her head, she told herself. So it was time to start thinking hard about the situation and a way out of it, now that she was alone and could concentrate.

Liam had left her there with polite but firm instructions to stay put, that someone would always be downstairs watching. And for all his joking and smiling, Hayley sensed the man meant what he said; there was a steel core beneath the young, affable exterior.

She doubted Quinn would have any other kind of man working for him.

And Quinn was obviously and indisputably the boss. She'd heard enough when he'd been in the doorway, giving orders with precision and decisiveness. Clearly all of the men followed his lead without question or hesitation. He was definitely the leader, and one who commanded respect.

Among other things, she thought. This would all be simpler if he wasn't so damned…impressive. A shiver rippled through her, a reaction she'd not had to any man in a very long time. That she was having it now was nothing short of infuriating.

But Teague's last words, about saluting someone who deserved it, stuck in her head. At first it had made her feel oddly comforted, until she realized it all depended on Teague's frame of reference. If he was a young, honestly idealistic sort, it could mean Quinn was a good guy.

But then it struck her that one of those zealots she'd thought about could use the same words about whatever leader had hit upon the right buttons to push. They could all be deluded, working for Quinn out of some misguided devotion to an idea. Or worse.

She got up, moving as silently as she could around the loft, looking. It was only about ten feet deep, but it ran the width of the entire cabin. Besides the chair, which sat next to a reading lamp, there was a double bed against the other side wall, a nightstand next to it and a low dresser against the back wall.

Under the window.

Her hopes leaped, but the moment she got close enough, she could see that the lack of morning light streaming through the window wasn't, as she'd hoped, simply because there were shutters she could open. It was because the window was solidly, carefully boarded over, just like most of those downstairs.

A quick test of the blockage told her there would be no budging it without some serious tools or a lot more strength than she had. Nor was there anything else in the room that she could use as a weapon.

Not, she thought wryly, that there was anything she could see herself using as a weapon against these obviously well-trained and dangerous men.

She sank down on the edge of the bed. Now that they had stopped moving, there was little left to distract her from the reality of her grim situation.

She wondered where Vicente was. There was room for a bedroom below this loft. Was that where he, as the primary—what? Guest? Prisoner?—was? The man had obviously been sincerely bothered, felt responsible somehow for getting her into this.

Although it was, she had to admit ruefully, mostly Cutter's fault. If he hadn't burst out of the trees like that, refusing to heed her recall, neither of them would be here. But it was so unlike the dog that she couldn't help thinking there was something else going on. While Cutter was an independent animal, he was also usually obedient, unless what she wanted him to do conflicted with something he knew he had to do.

That might sound odd to some, but she'd seen it too often in the months since he'd landed in her life. Like the time when he absolutely refused to come inside one night, and she'd had to go retrieve him physically from the side of the house. Only then did she notice the distinctive smell of propane, and realize that there was a dangerous leak. Or the time he'd literally dragged her outside into a pouring rain, then up the hill to where she'd found the neighbor who'd been pinned by a fallen tree, hurt and unable to reach his cell phone, and soaked through by the gush of water from the skies.

Water.

Had Quinn really meant he'd withhold water from Cutter? She couldn't believe anybody would do that to an innocent animal, but then she couldn't believe anybody would grab an innocent bystander—two, counting Cutter—and throw them onto a helicopter in the middle of the night and fly them off to who knows where and—

As if her thoughts had made him materialize, she heard the familiar click of toenails on the wood floor downstairs. And after a moment, she heard Quinn's voice.

"Take him upstairs. Tell her to keep him up there, out of the way."

There was another exchange she couldn't hear. Then, a moment later, she heard Teague laugh.

"He's not going anywhere for me, boss."

"So carry him."

"You seen his teeth?"

"Afraid of a pet dog?"

"Nope. Just doing what you've always said. Each man to the job he does best. The dog likes you, ergo, you do it."

There was a pause, then a sound that could have been a half-suppressed snort of laughter, or a not-at-all-suppressed sound of disgust.

She heard footsteps on the stairs. With an effort she stayed seated on the edge of the bed; for some reason it seemed important that he know she wasn't going to jump at his every appearance or command.

Moments later Cutter appeared at the top of the stairs and ran to her with every appearance of his usual delight at seeing her after time apart. Quinn was right behind him, but he stopped—thankfully—at the top of the stairs.

"*Now* you remember me," she muttered to the dog, not really meaning it as she gratefully scratched his ears. Cutter sighed and leaned against her.

She looked over at Quinn then. He was watching her steadily. An old joke flashed through her mind, about how the best way to make yourself feel insignificant was to try to give orders to someone else's dog. Obviously that didn't apply here. Or else Quinn was incapable of feeling insignificant.

Now, that I'd believe, she thought.

"You wouldn't really deny him water," she said, as if stating it as a fact instead of a question would get her the response she wanted.

"Wouldn't I?"

It had been a silly effort, she'd known that even as she'd said it.

Quinn moved farther into the loft, and she was reminded sharply how tall he was. The low roof that was still a good foot above her head was bare inches above his.

"Whether he drinks—or eats—is entirely up to you."

She blinked. "Me?"

"You behave, he gets what he needs."

The word "behave" nearly set her off; she didn't care for being spoken to as if she were a recalcitrant child. But she had to look out for Cutter now, not herself.

"You'd abuse an innocent animal to manipulate me?"

"I'm not convinced he's all that innocent," Quinn said, with a hint of something in his voice as he glanced at the dog— who seemed annoyingly happy at the moment—that sounded almost like amusement. Almost.

She challenged him, hoping he'd think she wasn't afraid of him. That mattered, for some reason. Never mind that inside she was practically quaking.

"What makes you think it will work?"

He shrugged. "You saw we were armed and you still came running after him."

She drew back slightly, looking up at him in genuine curiosity. "Why would you shoot an innocent woman chasing an even more innocent dog?"

"I didn't know you were innocent."

Something curled and knotted inside her. What kind of world did he live in, where the assumption was the opposite, where you were presumed guilty, or at the least a threat, until proved otherwise?

The kind of world that can put that look in someone's eyes, that coolness, that control, that world-weariness and distrust, she thought. His eyes weren't just blue, they had a tinge of ice.

"For all I knew you'd set him on us," he said.

That was so preposterous words burst from her. "Do you often get attacked by total strangers' dogs?"

He shrugged again. "It's happened."

"Hard to believe, you're so charming," she said, then wondered when she'd developed the habit of speaking before she thought.

But there it was again, that hint of a change in his face that could, if you stretched your imagination a bit, be amusement.

"And you," he added, almost conversationally, "charged armed men. Given the circumstances, the wise thing, the thing most people would have done, was turn tail and get as far away as they could. But you—"

"So I'm an idiot. Fine," she said, bitterly aware it was true.

"You love him." His gaze flicked to Cutter, then back to her. "Enough to charge into figurative hell for him."

"And that makes me easy to manipulate."

"Among other things, yes."

She didn't want to know what those "other things" were. Anybody who'd use a dog, threaten to starve it, wasn't starting out in a good place with her.

Not that it mattered. It would work. She couldn't do anything, risk anything, because he just might be cold enough to do exactly what he'd said. And if she made him angry enough, there was that gun....

Although killing Cutter—she swallowed as the words went through her rattled mind—would lose him his lever.

"You said he could be helpful." Even she heard the undertone of desperation in her voice.

"He already has been," Quinn admitted. "But we've survived this long without a dog on the team, I think we can make it a bit longer."

"What 'team'? Who are you?"

The thought that she was better off not knowing made her regret the question as soon as it was out.

"Right now, we're the ones in charge of you, and your dog. You should remember that."

Another threat? It took every bit of nerve she had left to meet his warning gaze. It seemed important somehow, not to cower in front of this man, even if that was what she felt like doing.

But she couldn't fight them. Couldn't fight him. She had no weapons, not enough strength or knowledge, and even if she could get free, there was that middle-of-nowhere thing to deal with.

No, it was in her and her dog's best interest to...just behave.

And she hated that she was scared enough to decide to do just that.

Chapter Nine

"Boss?"

Quinn snapped out of his musings about the woman upstairs and turned to look at Liam. The young man was also their IT guy, or as he jokingly called himself, their propeller head. He had his laptop, a rugged, rubber-bumpered version that was utilized by many military operations, set up on the coffee table in the center of the room.

His skill with computers, matched with a surprising skill with weapons and physical toughness, was a prized combination Quinn had been glad to find, even if it had come with the beginnings of a police record. But Liam had taken to their work with dedication and flair; all he'd needed was a purpose.

"You need to take a look at this."

Quinn looked up from the status report—they had another team on a secondary mission—he'd been reading on his smartphone, aided by the cell tower they themselves had installed, disguising it much as they had the cabin, inside the weathered, broken-looking windmill.

If Liam said he had something worth looking at, he did;

the man was a master at tracking, in both the real and cyber worlds. And he also understood what some didn't, that checking your back trail could sometimes be as important as checking the trail ahead.

"What is it?" he asked as he walked over to look at the laptop screen.

"Found this on a local news station out of Seattle."

Quinn leaned in to look at the video embedded beneath a large headline that read "One Feared Dead After Explosion, House Fire."

Back trail it was, Quinn thought as he looked at the video. He read the first paragraph of the story.

"I'm pretty sure—" Liam began.

"It is," Quinn agreed.

"They're saying the explosion could have been propane."

"Logical assumption. There was a tank."

They both knew better.

"It says the explosion was reported just after 0100 hours," Liam said. "We lifted off at 0032 hours, so they were right on our tail. Minus a few minutes for them to set up whatever they blew it with, that's less than a half-hour margin."

"Close."

"Way too close. There's no way they should have been able to pull that off."

"They shouldn't have been able to find him in the first place."

"You think we've been compromised?"

"You think that—" Quinn gestured at the laptop "—is coincidence? That an empty house just happened to blow up within a half hour of us being there?"

"No, sir. I don't believe in coincidence any more than you do."

"Occam's razor, Liam."

"What?"

"If you have to work too hard to make another theory fit, it's probably wrong."

Quinn took his cell phone out again, and keyed in the message he hated having to send.

"We're going dark?"

"We are," Quinn said grimly. It cut them off from all information and help, but he had no choice until they were able to set up secure communications again.

"We have a leak?" Liam sounded disbelieving; Quinn liked his faith in their own people.

"Someone does," Quinn said, and sent the signal that shut them down.

Hayley backed silently away from the edge of the loft and sat on the edge of the bed. Her legs were a little cramped from crouching there so long, peering over the railing down into the living room. Cutter followed, and jumped up on the bed beside her.

She wondered if the men below had heard her. She hadn't been able to hear much of what they'd said, since they had their backs to her. And only when Quinn had moved aside to take out his complicated-looking smartphone had she been able to see the laptop screen.

She'd barely managed to suppress a gasp of shocked horror at what she'd seen. She'd only been able to read the blaring headline on the news site from up here, but the accompanying video had begun by showing the road in front of the location, and then the distinctive peaked roof of her neighbor's house. Engulfed in flames that shot toward a dark sky.

The headline had said one was feared dead, yet she knew her neighbor was here, alive and well. And as far as she knew, he'd lived alone.

As far as she knew.

All sorts of wild scenarios began to race through her head; had there been another person living there? Had the person died in the fire? Or was he or she already dead? Was her quiet, reclusive neighbor really a killer, hiding some poor soul in that house, and—

Cutter let out a small sound and squirmed slightly; she'd tightened her grip on him too much, tugging on his fur.

"Sorry," she whispered to the dog.

In case someone came up to investigate the sound, she lifted her feet up to lie on the bed, where she had been before she'd decided to take a look downstairs. She'd been futilely trying to rest with some idea her mind might sharpen up enough to figure a way out of this if she just got some sleep.

But everything had shifted now. Had they set some kind of bomb, to blow the place up after they'd left? With someone still inside? Quinn had come out a few minutes after Vicente and Teague, so perhaps he'd set it himself. Which would make him...a murderer.

Of course, the headline had said "feared dead." Maybe they just didn't know yet, maybe they were assuming it was her neighbor, since they obviously wouldn't be able to find him.

She wouldn't have thought things could get more ominous than they already were. But somehow the idea that they had destroyed that quirky house that had stood for over half a century, just to cover their tracks, made it worse.

But had they? The only two words she was certain she'd heard from up here were "explosion" and "leak."

Had it been an accident?

In a house that had had propane for years without incident, precisely when all this had happened?

Her own thoughts rang with such sarcasm in her mind that she chastised herself for being fool enough to even consider the idea. She might not live in Quinn's world, whatever it was, but even she couldn't believe in that much coincidence.

On the comfortable bed, her tired body at last succumbed to sleep. But her mind never surrendered, and treated her to a string of nightmare scenarios that made the sleep anything but restful. And on some level, in that strange way of dreams, her mind knew that what it was producing was no more frightening than the reality she was going to wake up to.

Chapter Ten

Hayley awoke with a start. And alone; Cutter had vanished. Under the circumstances, it was disconcerting to think the dog had slipped out of her grasp without waking her, jumped off the bed without waking her and apparently gotten down the stairs without waking her.

She sat up, looking around to make sure the dog hadn't simply decamped to the floor. It was still full daylight, but she sensed she must have slept at least a couple of hours, maybe three. It was starting to get a bit warm up here in the loft, which made her think it must be afternoon by now. And that perhaps Cutter had headed down to cooler environs; that dense, double coat of his made him well suited for the cool, rainy Northwest, but not so much for this hotter clime, wherever it was.

She got up and walked as quietly as she could to the edge of the loft and looked over. There was no one in sight. Even the laptop that had displayed the video that had unsettled her sleep was gone.

As was her dog.

She hoped Cutter hadn't irritated the already irascible Quinn. Although he'd seemed much more kindly disposed toward Cutter than her. The dog, he'd admitted, could be useful.

And unless you were utterly stone cold, it was pretty hard to ignore a dog who took a liking to you. She didn't want to know the person who could look at those bright eyes, lolling tongue and happy tail and walk away without even a smile.

But she wasn't sure she liked the idea of her dog being useful to a bunch of armed men of uncertain purpose. That kind of usefulness often didn't end well.

Cutter's instincts about people were almost supernaturally accurate. In fact, she couldn't think of an occasion—until now—that they had failed. It had been the dog who had led her to make overtures to crusty Mr. Elkhart from the library, who, as it turned out, had merely been a lonely old man who had always relied on his late wife to break the ice with people. He was also, she'd found to her awe, a war hero who had come home from Korea with a box of medals and stories that made her marvel at where such men came from. And, even more surprising, he was an artist of no small talent. The quick charcoal sketch he'd done of Cutter hung in a place of honor in her study.

The image of the drawing hit her unexpectedly hard, and it took her a moment to realize she was wondering if she'd ever see it again. What would happen if she never came back? There was no one left in the family except for some cousins in Missouri whom she rarely saw, and of course Walker, her wandering brother. She wasn't even sure where he was just now. She hadn't heard from him in nearly a month. But she knew he wouldn't want the house. She didn't think Walker was ever going to settle in one place. Never had anyone been more appropriately named.

And she was ginning up chaos in her head again, thinking of any and everything but the situation she was in. And that needed to change. Now.

Steeling herself, she crept quietly down the stairs. Surely

they didn't expect her to stay up there all the time? Quinn had ordered her to stay except for bathroom runs, but maybe he wasn't here right now. Besides, if they really meant it strictly, wouldn't they have tied her up or something?

She shivered at the idea. Maybe they would, if she poked around too much. That they hadn't, while encouraging, did little to relieve her fears.

When she got to the bottom of the narrow stairs, she saw Liam in the kitchen, drinking from a bottle of water. The young man smiled at her, looking oddly apologetic.

"Hi," he said, as if she were just an ordinary guest. He lifted the bottle. "There's more in the fridge."

Was that an invitation? She walked toward him cautiously.

"I thought water was an issue."

"Just from the well. It's never failed, but it's kind of slow. You can't use a lot at once." The young man smiled again, more normally this time. "No twenty-minute showers, I'm afraid."

"But now there's me. And my dog. Where is he, by the way?"

"We tend to overstock, so we'll be okay, and if we run low, there are options. And your dog is out with Quinn. He's out on watch. We stagger them. I'm hydrating because I'm his relief in ten minutes."

"He takes a watch?"

Liam shrugged. "He doesn't ask anybody to do what he won't do himself."

"You sound…admiring."

Liam looked puzzled. "Of course. I wouldn't work for him if I didn't admire him. He pulled me off a bad path. He's the best boss I've ever had."

For a guy who looked so young he could have been flipping burgers at a fast-food place not so long ago, Hayley wasn't sure that was saying much.

"Oh, that reminds me. He left some stuff for you in the bathroom."

Hayley blinked. "Stuff?"

"Pair of sweats, a T-shirt, that kind of thing. To wear while those—" he gestured with the water bottle "—are in the wash."

She was so startled it took her a moment to process. "Quinn did that?"

Unlike his boss, Liam's smile broke free. Was it just that he was younger, or that he hadn't been at this—whatever "this" was—as long?

"He's not nearly as bad as he comes across. He's just all business, all the time."

All the time?

She managed to stop the question before it came out, realizing ahead of time—for once—what it might sound like.

"So," she said instead, "is that part of the overstocking, extra clothes? And what wash?"

Liam grinned then, and for the moment looked like any ordinary guy. If it hadn't been for the weapon on his hip.

"Let's just say we have the best logistics person on the planet. Thinks of everything." He pointed toward the bathroom. "And there's a small washer and dryer in the closet opposite the bathroom."

Since he seemed open enough, Hayley decided to risk something she instinctively would never try with Quinn. "What on earth is going on? Who *are* you guys?"

As quickly as that, the easy demeanor was gone, vanished behind the brisk, professional manner.

"You'll have to talk to Quinn about that."

"And I'm sure he'll answer loquaciously," she said drily.

"Quinn," Liam said, with a glint of humor returning to his eyes for a moment, "doesn't do *anything* loquaciously."

"Now there's a surprise."

Hayley was startled at her own snarkiness. She was being held by armed men of unknown intent. She should be thinking of survival, not mouthing off and inviting a smackdown.

She studied Liam a moment, finding it hard to believe that open, boy-next-door face would be involved in something as nefarious as this seemed to be.

"Question is," she murmured, almost to herself, "is his hat black or white?"

"Oh, definitely white. He's the goodest of the good guys," Liam quipped, then snapped his mouth shut, as if he regretted speaking so impulsively. Or perhaps that he'd talked so much at all.

He finished his water quickly, said a goodbye that was just as quick and started to walk away. She wished she felt more reassured than she did by his quick, heartfelt response. But she wasn't a fool. She knew that many people who did crazy, even evil things thought they were in the right. From eco-terrorists to the international variety, from black-swathed anarchists to fist-clenching Marxists, they were all convinced their cause was right.

She heard steps on the porch before Liam got to the door, and realized only then that he must have heard someone coming. Something she hadn't heard at all. Then she realized she should have known; they would never leave her here alone, unguarded, so he would never have started to leave unless he knew someone else was coming.

She'd doubled their workload, she realized. They not only had to watch for whatever outside threat they were worried about, they had to worry about her. If they were somewhere where escape might do her some good, she could use it as a tool, but not out here, where it seemed there was no possible help for miles, miles she couldn't cross without supplies, especially water, if she could at all. She was in decent shape, but she had the feeling an escape would require a lot more than decent.

It would require someone in as good condition as these men were.

On the thought, the primest specimen of the four of them walked in. Quinn spoke briefly to Liam, who nodded and left. She wondered where the other two men were. Staggered shifts, Liam had said. So one person at least was always out there, watching? That would fit; Quinn obviously ran a tight operation.

And then Cutter came through the door, spotted her and dashed across the room with his usual joyous greeting.

"Have you stayed out of trouble?" she asked the dog as she bent to pet him, paying special attention to that spot below his right ear that he loved having scratched long and hard. She couldn't really blame the dog, after all; he was an independent spirit, and why stay cooped up if you didn't have to? Although she still found his sudden attraction to Quinn decidedly unsettling.

Almost as unsettling as her own. Because she couldn't deny the way her pulse leaped every time she saw him, and how her breath caught every time those cool blue eyes focused on her. And it was getting harder and harder to convince herself it was simply out of fear.

"He's a smart dog," Quinn said.

"Usually," she agreed.

If he caught the veiled jab, he didn't respond. "I gather he doesn't usually…react this way to strangers?"

"He usually has better judgment, yes."

This time one corner of his mouth twitched slightly. Hayley remembered her earlier thought about the imprudence of her smart mouth. She mellowed her tone.

"Are you sure he wasn't yours once? Maybe in another life?"

"I'm sure. In either life," Quinn said.

He walked toward the bedroom in back, where, as far as she could tell, her once-neighbor was ensconced with no desire to emerge.

Hayley stood still, trying to figure out what he'd meant by "either life." For that matter, what he meant by anything.

And realizing she could spend all her time trying to figure out the man called Quinn, and never get any closer to the truth.

Chapter Eleven

Always watch the head of the snake.

She'd heard that, somewhere, some nature show. Or maybe one of the documentaries on a military operation she watched when she needed to believe there were still heroes in the world. Either way, it made sense. So she watched Quinn. And it wasn't as if looking at him was any sort of a hardship. And when he wasn't there, she asked about him. What else was she going to do?

But it was odd, she mused. All four men here, excluding the still-reclusive Vicente, were tough, strong—and handsome, in a hard-jawed sort of way—young men. Yet it was Quinn who still drew her eye.

Hayley shifted the pillow behind her back. She'd managed to convince Teague to let her stay downstairs, promising to restrict herself to the bathroom and the seating area by the fireplace. When Quinn had returned from his patrol outside a few minutes ago—Cutter at his heels—she'd half expected him to order her back upstairs. And he did give Teague a sharp look.

"I showed her the bookshelf. She's been reading the whole

time I've been here," the man explained, then hastily retreated to the other side of the room before Quinn could…what? Take his head off? For telling the truth?

Because it was true. She'd been surprised at the eclectic selection of books hidden behind one of the sliding doors in the hallway. The top shelves held nonfiction, biographies and history, and fiction, short stories from Hemmingway to Daoul, and novels from Twain and Austen to today's Roberts and Flynn. There were other volumes in Spanish, French and a couple of other languages she didn't recognize.

They had about every taste covered, she thought, and had suddenly realized that was likely the goal, if they used this place for this sort of thing often. Which they must, or it wouldn't be so well organized and stocked. The realization didn't make her feel any better.

But the thought that they had provided books to read oddly did, a little. Especially given the lack of television or any computer except their own. Security precaution, no doubt; they could follow any news of their doings, but their victims were kept in the dark.

She noticed the lower two shelves were full of young adult and kids' books to cover a wide gamut of budding tastes. She saw at one end the familiar wizard books. Smiling, she reached for the first one and lifted it from the shelf. She wouldn't mind reading it again, or all of them, for that matter. She could use a bit of escapism at the moment.

Yeah, since it's as close to escape as you're going to get, she thought sourly. *Gee, maybe you'll have time to read them all before you get out of here.*

If she got out of here, she amended silently.

Belatedly, the significance of the presence of kids' books down to the picture book level, on the bottom shelf, hit her. They brought children here?

That thought rattled her almost more than anything else had, and all the time she sat reading the exploits of three smart, nervy and, yes, noble kids, she was wondering about the children who must have passed through here. Were they still alive, or had their lives been cut short, as witnesses it was too dangerous to let live?

Tough as they were, she couldn't picture any of these men cold-bloodedly murdering a child, but she also knew her brain probably couldn't wrap around the idea anyway.

Cutter's leap up into her lap jerked her out of her reverie and back to the present. She had to watch that, she thought as she hugged the dog. It wouldn't do to get so lost in thought, especially around Quinn. She needed her wits about her with him. With all of them, really, but especially with him.

Now, he had disappeared down the hallway toward the bedroom. She heard voices; he was having some sort of conversation with Vicente. She got up, signaling Cutter to wait, not wanting his toenails on the floor to give her away, not that Quinn needed the warning since he seemed to have eyes in the back of his head anyway. She headed for the kitchen, slowly, as quietly as she could manage. She got a bottle of water from the small fridge, taking her time about it.

Listening.

"—will not do it."

"Vicente, listen to me. Do you want these guys to win—"

"I want *you* to do the job you were hired to do. You are the best, correct?"

"We will. We are. But there are no guarantees."

"If I do what you ask, they who want it will have no need of me. No reason to keep me alive."

"That's not true—"

"You are a good man. I respect you. But I will not do it."

Quinn let out an exasperated sound. A split second later Hayley realized the conversation was over, and she darted out of the kitchen, hoping he'd been too focused on what had apparently been a futile attempt at persuasion to either hear or worry about what she was doing in the kitchen. She scurried back to her spot on the couch, making sure her fresh water bottle was visible.

What was it Vicente had refused to do? Whatever it was, Quinn hadn't forced him to do it. In fact, he had deferred to the man's decision. Of course, one thing was clear. They'd been hired to do this, whatever "this" was. Were they simply incredibly well-equipped bodyguards, was that all this was? Was Vicente in some kind of trouble, so big he needed such elaborate protection? Who was it who needed him alive now, but no longer would if he did whatever it was Quinn had asked of him?

She tried hard to keep her mind focused on all of those questions, so that it wouldn't hover over the one statement that had jolted her the most.

You are a good man. I respect you.

Was he? Didn't the perception of what was a good man depend on who was doing the looking? Having the respect of, say, an upstanding citizen was one thing, but having the respect of some street thug was something else entirely.

Quinn came back into the room, stopping for a moment just past the kitchen entryway. She realized he was staring at her, perhaps assessing if he should give that order for her to get back upstairs. She wondered that she had ever thought she'd seen a trace of softening in this man; he was brusque, cool, unemotional and not the least inclined to explain himself or anything else to her. He was utterly focused on his mission, and she a mere—and minor—distraction.

"Interesting choice," he said, looking at her book.

There was no more emotion in his words than if he'd been checking off an item on a list. So if he thought her silly to be reading what was pushed as a book for kids, it certainly didn't show.

"Escape," she said shortly, well aware of the multiple ways he could interpret that answer. And yet again she questioned the wisdom of it, after the fact.

Think before *you speak, that's the way it's supposed to go,* she chided herself.

She turned her gaze back to her book, hoping if she appeared to be simply reading, and not making any trouble, he would let her stay and not banish her to the loft. She nearly laughed inwardly at the idea that he might be courteous enough not to want to disturb someone's reading. Especially one of his captives.

It was hard not to look up at him again. She could feel him studying her. In a way, the intensity, the alertness, the sense of a mission reminded her of Cutter. The dog exhibited the same sort of single-mindedness sometimes, the same sort of prowess at filtering priorities; that squirrel scampering past might be tempting, but he kept his focus on the larger goal, be it Mrs. Kerry's haughty gray cat or some bigger intruder.

Maybe that's why the darn dog was so enamored, she thought. He sensed a kindred spirit. The object of his attention clearly wasn't so sure; Quinn appeared more bemused than anything at the dog's attitude.

At last she heard him move, and a quick glance told her he'd walked over to Teague, and they were conversing quietly, too quietly for her to hear.

After a few moments, despite the gripping story, she gave up on trying to read. It simply wasn't possible with Quinn in the room. The energy he brought with him was as tangible as gravity, and when he walked in, everything shifted.

As did Cutter. He slipped off the sofa and made a beeline for his new idol.

Quinn, listening to Teague now, didn't seem to notice the dog at all, but Hayley suspected he knew exactly when the dog had begun to move. He seemed hyperaware of everything around him. He'd have to be, she supposed, if he did this kind of thing often. She didn't want to think about that, about the others who might have been through here, others who might have been—

Her thoughts were interrupted sharply by a simple, almost absent motion from Quinn. What would be a completely natural action, under normal circumstances. But now, under these circumstances, from this man, it stopped her breath.

Without even looking he reached down and scratched Cutter's right ear.

She stared as the dog wiggled in delight, then leaned against

Quinn's leg. Quinn still didn't look at him, but the gentle, affectionate caress continued. And the dog sighed happily.

This couldn't be the first time, unless Quinn had somehow magically guessed that was the exact spot Cutter loved, just behind and below his right ear.

Hayley stared, unable to look away. And telling herself it meant nothing didn't help. She knew it was silly, even foolish, but she felt reassured. Quinn might be cool, efficient and unapproachable, but apparently he wasn't untouchable.

Teague made a gesture in her general direction. Quinn glanced at her, then shook his head.

The chill that swept her washed away the tiny bit of reassurance she'd felt at his kindly gesture toward the dog. Obviously, she had become a topic of discussion, and the realization made her very nervous.

It was foolish, really. She'd read too much into that one gesture. Even evil men in history had had dogs they apparently cared for, hadn't they? It was people they didn't give a damn about, and while she could list several reasons why animals might be preferable, it was still a very unsettling thought.

She realized with a little jolt that she was staring at him, transfixed. And as if he felt it, he looked at her again. This time it was more than just a glance. It was a steady gaze, and she felt her heart start to thud heavily in her chest.

She made herself look back at her book, more than a little frightened at how hard it was.

Telling herself it was all part of observing him, of learning about him for her own safety, was one thing.

Believing it was, apparently, something else altogether.

Chapter Twelve

This had the potential, Quinn thought, to degenerate into a complete FUBAR.

Hell, it already is beyond all recognition, he muttered inwardly as the dog trotted happily at his side. That sure as hell was never in the plan.

Cutter came to a halt suddenly, and half turned. Instinctively Quinn stopped as well, wondering what had drawn the dog's attention.

"Hey, boss."

Rafer's voice came softly out of the darkness from behind him, making Quinn feel both satisfied and worried. Satisfied because he'd never heard Rafer's approach; the man was good. Worried because he'd never heard Rafer's approach; he himself was obviously a screwup.

Or far too distracted.

"All clear?" he asked.

"Yes, sir. All quiet. Teague's on the southern perimeter, he says the same." Rafer glanced at the dog. "He sure makes it hard to sneak up on anybody."

Except me, apparently, Quinn thought. "Noted. He's handy. Go on and get some rest. I'll take it now."

"You're not due for forty-five minutes yet."

"And yet here I am," Quinn muttered. "Go." *Somebody might as well get some rest, and it obviously isn't going to be me.*

"Yes, sir."

Quinn started walking again, and the dog immediately took up the same position at his side.

Maybe it's a damned good thing the mutt is here, he thought, *since you've got your head so far up—*

Cutter made a low, whuffing kind of sound, quartered to the right and picked up the pace. Quinn realized in that moment the very slight breeze had shifted, and wondered if the change had brought the dog some new scent.

Then he saw a movement far off to his right. Teague, he guessed, in the second before the man flashed the all-clear arm signal. Quinn returned it. The dog halted, as if he had understood the signal, that it meant all was well. The animal trotted back and took up his position at Quinn's side.

Maybe it *was* a good thing, having a dog around. Especially one as smart as this one seemed to be. He'd worked with K-9 units before, and while they'd always amazed him, he'd never thought about adding one to their staff. But this dog, who he'd first assumed was all beauty and little brain, was rapidly proving him wrong. For a dog with no military or law enforcement training, he either had incredible instincts, or was learning so fast it was uncanny.

That is, assuming he hadn't had any of that training. He had never actually asked that question of the dog's owner.

...Hayley, not that you bothered to ask.

He had the feeling she wouldn't have stayed anonymous for long anyway. He'd had to deal with other types of women in these situations before, and many of them became nearly non-functional. Certainly few had ever held on to the nerve to get up in his grill the way this one did. He had to grant her that, she wasn't lacking nerve.

Nor, he thought wryly, several other attributes the other men hadn't failed to notice. And with the intuition that was part of the reason they were working for him, they all unerringly seemed to realize that this woman was somehow getting under his skin.

The jokes hadn't degenerated into crude masculine teasing. They often dealt with a more fragile sort of woman who might be genuinely hurt by such jesting. Or worse, one who would take serious offense and probably spread the word at the first opportunity; that kind of notoriety was not helpful. So it was easier to never do it, than to remember not to when they were within earshot of said females.

Or just stay away from them. That was always good.

And so here he was. And he wasn't happy about that, either. Had he, Quinn Foxworthy, really passed up on the opportunity for enough sleep to continue to function at his preferred level, just to get out and away from that smart-mouthed, too-clever woman with the eyes the color of a grassy meadow?

And when the hell did you start thinking in similes?

He swore at himself sharply. If he kept this up, he was going to make some stupid, rookie mistake, simply because he was too damned distracted to keep his head in the game. So things had gone a bit awry, but hadn't he always preached flexibility? Hadn't he lectured time and again on the fluid nature of their work, how you had to be ready without warning to respond to rapidly changing conditions? So why the hell wasn't he taking his own advice? Why was he so rattled over this?

It was her own fault. That's what you got when you wandered around in isolated woods at midnight. She should have stayed home and let the dog find his own way back. Obviously he was smart enough to do so.

More than smart enough; whatever annoyance his owner might bring, the dog was proving anything but a hindrance. Quinn could see coming to trust the animal's much more powerful ears and nose. It wouldn't take much, he guessed, to turn him into a top-notch service dog.

He wondered if she'd sell him.

He nearly chuckled aloud at the image that flashed through his head at his own question. Judging by the way she looked at him, she'd probably figured he'd just appropriate the dog. He hadn't missed the moments, usually right after she'd come back at him with some smart remark, when fear had flashed through her eyes. The moments when, too late, her common sense must have kicked in and reminded her it might be wiser to stay quiet.

He should be grateful for that fear, he told himself. If she stayed quiet, maybe he could keep her out of his mind. He had the discipline, hard-won. He just had to apply it, that's all.

But the memory of that look of fear in her eyes stayed with him. Bothered him. It pushed at him, prodded, until he almost sent the dog back to her just to get rid of the reminder.

He wondered if the animal would go if he told him to. He seemed to make a lot of his own decisions, and while he vanished regularly to check on her, he always returned, as if he'd decided this, too, was his job.

"You should be riding herd on her, not me," he muttered to the dog. Eerily, as if he truly had understood, the dog looked at the cabin, and then back at him. If he'd spoken the words he couldn't have said more clearly "She's safe inside."

"You're almost spooky, you know that?"

Cutter watched him intently, those dark eyes again putting him in mind of a herding dog who controlled his animals by sheer force of the will pouring out of those eyes.

The dog walked forward a few steps, then turned back, clearly waiting for him to continue. After a moment he did, shaking his head wryly, wondering who was really running this duty shift.

FUBAR, he thought again. Making rounds with a dog had never been in the plan.

Nor had having to fight to keep his mind off that dog's person. He didn't want her scared, he thought. He just wanted her gone. Wanted her never to have shown up last night.

And that kind of hopeless, helpless wishing was something

that he'd thought had been blasted out of him by real life decades ago.

Yes, things were definitely FUBAR.

The only question was, did it apply to the plan, or just to him?

Chapter Thirteen

Hayley woke up with a start. For a moment the dream lingered, so vivid and real that she actually turned to look at the wall beside the bed. In the dream she'd begun tracking the days in that old, clichéd way, by making hash marks on the wall. She'd been using the handle of the razor she'd snagged from the bathroom, which had so far in reality proved as useless as she'd feared.

But that wasn't what made her shiver now. It was the image in her mind from the dream, so clear and sharp she was almost surprised the wall she was staring at was untouched.

She sat up slowly, wrapping her arms around herself, feeling as if the room were much colder than it probably was. She didn't know where they were, but it was warm during the day, and downright chilly at night. Someone started a fire in the fireplace every evening, with what Teague had told her were energy logs, made of sawdust and wood chips compressed into solid, round logs that burned hotter, cleaner and longer than any natural log. It kept it nicely warm up here where the heat collected.

When she'd asked Teague why not use the also-efficient furnace, he'd explained this saved propane from the big tank in the barn for other operations—cooking, heating water and, most important, generating electricity.

He'd seemed so willing to talk she'd risked asking how long they were going to be here. And he'd instantly clammed up, excusing himself abruptly. He hadn't even explained that he couldn't talk about it. He simply ignored her question and left.

The image from her dream shot through her mind again.

Four sets of five hash marks, followed by the one she'd been making in the dream. Twenty-one days.

Twenty-one days. Three weeks.

The thought that she might still be sitting here in three weeks—or even longer—was horrible to contemplate. Three days had been bad enough.

The alternative, however, was worse.

She kept telling herself that. As the hours crept by and she was still alive, she found herself thinking maybe they weren't going to kill her. After all, if they were going to, why not do it now and avoid the hassle of feeding and sharing water with her? As Quinn had so pointedly observed, Cutter was at least useful. She was just...

What? A nuisance? An annoyance?

She shook her head sharply. She was nothing so mild, and she'd better remember that. She was a witness, an unwanted witness to a kidnapping. And then a victim of abduction herself. And none of that added up to her simply walking away and going home unscathed when this was over.

Yet her mind kept trying to convince itself that was possible. Teague seemed like a nice guy, with a bright sense of humor that surprised her. Liam seemed so young and innocent she couldn't figure out why he was doing this. Rafer was quiet, almost withdrawn, with shadows in his eyes that she didn't think were totally due to what must have been a serious injury to his left leg; she'd been right about the limp, but it didn't seem to slow him down much.

As for her neighbor, he might as well be a ghost for all she'd seen of him. He had apparently taken Quinn's order to heart, since he'd made no effort to speak to her. And when they had happened to meet in the hallway near the bathroom last night, he had scuttled away as if she were somehow scarier than the men holding them.

Or as if he knew better than she the price for disobeying one of Quinn's orders.

Yeah, there was always that to be considered.

Not that the man had given her any orders beyond staying put. Good thing she wasn't prone to cabin fever, although she was starting to chafe at never being allowed outside. He didn't seem to be in the house much at all. He was always outside. Overseeing. Ordering.

And overachieving, no doubt. He seemed the type.

That was the downside to the relief of thinking they weren't going to kill her after all, at least not right away. Of course, they might just fly off and leave her here, out in the middle of a nowhere that for her truly was nowhere, since she had no idea where that nowhere was.

She groaned at her own tangled thoughts. That's all she seemed capable of lately, a confused bunch of ideas that seemed to chase each other's tails faster than Cutter could chase an unwary squirrel.

Light was growing in the loft. She had no clock, but obviously it was after dawn. That surprised her; she'd slept better than she expected, under the circumstances.

She heard the familiar sound of canine nails on the stairs. Cutter had been there last night when she went to bed, but had been gone once when she'd awoken in the night. She'd assumed, since it had become as much of a pattern as anything could in thirty-six hours, that he was with Quinn. The dog would accompany the other men if asked, but with Quinn, it was always so obviously the dog's decision that the other men laughed aloud. And he let them get away with it, giving only a wry quirk of his mouth in response.

The dog hopped up on the bed and presented her with a good-morning kiss.

"I wish you could talk," she said, hardly for the first time since the clever animal had dropped into her life. "I'd love to hear your explanation for this. Was he your person in another life? When he was maybe just a regular guy, an engineer or a software geek?"

"I prefer to think I was Sun Tzu."

She smothered a gasp; how did a man of his size manage to come up those stairs so quietly? And now that he was there, at the top of the stairs, looking at her, the last words she'd said echoed in her mind with a resounding silliness. This man, a software geek? Never happen. Too indoor. An engineer? Only if he was designing lethal weapons, she thought.

Sun Tzu, ancient warrior and author of *The Art of War?* Oh, yeah, she could see that.

For a long moment he just stood there, watching her. In fact, the few times he was inside when she was awake, he seemed to be doing just that, watching her.

Only to be expected, she told herself. After all, she watched him every second she could, and she knew he knew it. The man missed nothing. But she continued. The more she knew, the more chance she had of surviving this, right?

At least, that's how it had started out.

She remembered too clearly the moment yesterday when she'd realized something had changed. When she'd risked that Liam was engrossed enough in whatever information he was gleaning from that industrial-strength laptop not to notice her going over to peer out the one unboarded window at the front of the cabin, next to the intimidatingly large gun locker.

The scene that had met her eyes outside was as disconcerting as it was unexpected. Cutter, gleefully engaged in one of his favorite things in life, a serious game of fetch. Chasing a stick thrown again and again and again by an apparently equally tireless Quinn.

For an instant she had just stood there, staring, not at the dog but at the man. The man who moved so easily, so powerfully, with such tightly wound grace and strength. He threw that stick farther than she could ever have managed, and Cutter was loving it. It was a tableau that had made her chest tighten in a new, strange way that had nothing to do with fear and everything to do with the simple fact that Quinn was a very attractive man.

Now she began to move, intending to get to her feet, not liking the disadvantage of being in bed while he towered over her. But just in time she remembered she was clad only in the oversize T-shirt he'd found for her. It was all she could do not to grab the blanket and pull it up in front of her like the heroine of some old melodrama.

He'd still tower over you anyway, she muttered to herself, staying put.

"What do you want?" she snapped, her tone an effort to hide her agitation.

For an instant, the barest flash of a moment, Hayley thought she saw something flare in his eyes, something hot and tempting. But it was gone so instantly she would have thought she'd imagined it, if not for the sheer force of her own physical reaction; she nearly shivered.

"Supply run," he said simply. He shifted his gaze to the dog. "What does he need?"

"Going to helicopter to the nearest Walmart?"

"You might want to rethink the smart mouth when I'm asking what you might need."

"You asked what he needed."

"I like him."

"Because he doesn't ask questions?"

"Nor is he sarcastic."

She couldn't stop a rueful chuckle. "Oh, he can be, if he feels the need."

"Sarcastic? A dog?"

He was looking at her as she imagined he would one of those people who anthropomorphized their pets to extremes, attributing to them human thoughts and motivations as if the canine brain and the human brain were the same. She'd never been one of them, but Cutter...well, he was different. She supposed those other pet owners felt the same way, but Cutter really was.

"What would you call it when he howls whenever our frustrated-opera-singer mail carrier arrives?"

Quinn blinked. "What?"

"She's always singing, not very well. Flat at the top of her lungs, as it were. So Cutter took to announcing the mail delivery with a howl that sounds frighteningly like her. Complete with vibrato."

She was babbling about inanities now, but she supposed it was better than that sarcasm and making him angry at her. And he looked more bemused than angry as he looked at the dog sitting beside her on the bed. But then, he seemed bemused most of the time around the dog. And now, as Cutter looked back at him with that tongue-lolling, doggy grin, Hayley could swear she saw the corners of Quinn's mouth twitch as if he were fighting a return grin.

She wondered what he would look like if he ever cut loose that grin. He was devastating enough already, if he really opened up he'd be—

He'd still be the guy who kidnapped you.

She interrupted her own thoughts rather sternly. *You're supposed to be watching him to learn how to deal with him, to keep yourself alive, not noticing that he was annoyingly long, lean, dark and sexy.*

Although how she was supposed to overlook that she wasn't quite sure.

So don't overlook it, she ordered herself. *Just don't turn into a cliché here, the victim who falls for her kidnapper. Especially since you're just a sidelight here.*

"Why didn't you send Liam to ask, as usual?"

"He's sleeping. He had the late shift."

He said it negligibly, as if they were working in a factory or something, just ordinary men going about ordinary jobs. But there was nothing ordinary about what they were doing. And nothing ordinary about these men.

Especially the one standing in front of her, arms folded across his broad chest as he leaned against the loft railing.

She'd wondered who his boss was. Not just because he was so clearly the boss here, but also because she had a hard time picturing him taking orders from anybody. He took suggestions from his men, she'd seen that, and sometimes even acted on them, but orders from a superior? Even in her imagination, she just couldn't make it happen.

Her too-vivid imagination. The imagination that had her half convinced that every time he looked at her something turned over inside her. The imagination that fancied that something was growing larger, more consuming, with each passing hour.

Worst of all, the imagination that insisted there was some sort of answering heat in those intense eyes when he looked at her.

Oh, yeah, a walking cliché, that was her. And a fool.

And if she wasn't careful, she'd be a dead fool.

Chapter Fourteen

"She's just scared," Teague said.

Quinn stopped in the act of pouring coffee into a heavy mug and turned his head to look at the former marine. "Scared?"

Teague shrugged. "My sister was like that. When she got scared, she turned into a smart-ass. Lots of wisecracks, in your face, that kind of thing. I think it was her way to keep from getting hysterical."

His eyes went suddenly distant, as if looking at a scene far away. Quinn knew, too well, what vision had formed in the young man's mind. But he didn't comment; they'd had that discussion once before, and Quinn knew if Teague had his way, they never would again.

"She's asking a lot of questions," Teague said now. "Maybe we should tell her."

Quinn lifted a brow.

"I mean, she seems…pretty sane, and smart, maybe she'd understand," he said.

"Smart enough to pick you as the one to question," Quinn

said, making Teague grimace. "Don't," Quinn said at the expression.

"That's me, the nice guy on the team," Teague said wryly.

"One of the reasons you're here," Quinn pointed out. "And you know smart doesn't equal common sense."

Teague shrugged. "I know. Most of my college profs proved that. It's why I joined the marines."

Quinn's mouth quirked. Teague definitely had a good helping of both smart and common sense, not always the best recipe for academic survival these days.

"We can't take the chance, Teague. Too much depends on keeping this operation secret."

The man didn't argue, just nodded. That common sense kicking in, Quinn thought. He just wished their extra guest had enough to keep her mouth shut.

"Uh…boss?"

Something had shifted in Teague's tone, and an extra wariness changed his posture.

"Yeah, I know," Quinn said. "She's eavesdropping."

He heard the tiny gasp from behind him, just outside the kitchen entryway. Teague glanced that way, then back at Quinn's face.

"I'm going to go see what Vicente needs before I head out," he said quickly, and vanished.

Quinn was a little surprised when, instead of retreating after being caught out, their eavesdropper pressed forward. Whether Teague's assessment was right or not, she certainly wasn't lacking in nerve.

He watched as she took a mug from the rack, poured her own cup of coffee. Then she turned to face him, only the slightest ripple in the surface of the dark liquid hinting that she wasn't quite as cool as she seemed on the outside.

"What did you expect?" she asked.

She had, he conceded, a point. He just hadn't expected her to confront him with it, or so openly admit what she'd been doing.

"Knowledge is power," he said in acknowledgment.

"You'd do the same, if you were in my position. Not," she added, a note more wry than bitter coming into her voice, "that you would have allowed yourself to be kidnapped in the first place."

He studied her for a moment. "Although I dispute the word 'kidnap,' you didn't have much choice in the matter."

"What," she said, her tone turning sour, "would you call it?"

"A strategic decision."

She studied him in turn. And again, if he was judging strictly from the steady way she held his gaze, he would have said she wasn't scared at all. Only her protective body language, with the mug of hot coffee held as if it were a weapon, and the slight tremors that sent ripples through the dark liquid, gave her away.

"Well, your *strategic decision* sure looked and felt like a kidnapping from here."

"I'm sure it did."

Her brows lowered. "Don't patronize me, on top of everything else."

"Patronize?"

"Don't agree with me just to shut me up."

"I was agreeing with you because what you said was true. I'm sure it did seem like that to you."

She was looking at him as if she didn't trust a word he was saying. And he couldn't really blame her for that, either.

He began to gather things; skillet, eggs, bacon.

"Who are you guys?"

He hadn't expected that, either, a blunt, straightforward question. Maybe she wasn't as scared as Teague thought. Or maybe she just had enough grit and nerve to get past it.

"Right now," he said, "we're the guys who control things."

"You mean your guns control things."

"Just balance them."

"Balance?" Her voice went up a little, the first vocal betrayal of her nerves.

"'God made man, Sam Colt made them equal,' is how the saying goes, I believe."

She grimaced. "That was a different time," she said, and with a glance at his holstered sidearm added, "and that is not a Colt."

He didn't react to her unexpected knowledge, but he filed away the fact that she recognized the weapon; his handgun of choice was generally an H&K unless the job called for something else.

"A different time, yes," he agreed as he got out a bowl. "But people, they haven't changed much, not under the surface veneer of civilization."

"If that's supposed to be reassuring, it's not."

"It should be," he said. "We need tough people for tough times."

"If we need thugs and kidnappers, we're in more trouble than we can get out of," she retorted.

Quinn couldn't help it, he chuckled. He caught himself and kept it inward, but he realized with a little jolt that he liked the way she got in his face, came back at him despite her fear.

He started breaking eggs into the bowl. When he passed six, her brow furrowed. "Good thing they found out eggs aren't as bad for you as they thought."

He glanced at her. "Worried about my health?"

"Aren't you?"

"No, since this isn't just for me."

She blinked. "You're cooking breakfast for everybody?"

"Everybody takes their turn."

"Even you?"

He lifted a brow. "You'd rather I assigned it to you?"

"Depends. Any rat poison around?"

This time he didn't manage to keep the chuckle suppressed. "Sorry. Wanna come after me with this?" He lifted the large, heavy cast-iron skillet.

"Please, not another cliché," she muttered.

A third chuckle threatened. Which in itself amazed him. He couldn't remember the last time he'd felt this close to laughing, even once, let alone three times. But between her and her dog, he was grinning—albeit inwardly—a lot. That was disconcerting. He put the large skillet on a burner, and while it was heating he turned his focus to scrambling the eggs in the bowl and adding some seasonings.

"People will be looking for me by now. Probably him, too," she said as she gestured toward the bedroom where their prize prisoner seemed content to hide for the duration, coming out only for meals and the bathroom.

"Oh, people are looking for him, all right. You? Maybe. But you haven't exactly been a social butterfly since your mother passed away."

He flicked a glance at her in time to see her jaw drop. She stared at him, clearly stunned by his knowledge.

"How did you know about my mother?"

"We do our homework."

"And who the hell is 'we'?" she demanded. "Who are you people?"

He ignored that. Not that it stopped her.

"I've been thinking. You're either some huge criminal operation, or you must be the government in some way."

"Some," he said as he added some salt and pepper to the eggs, "would say there's not much difference."

"Government, I think," she said, as if he hadn't spoken. "They're the only ones who'd think you can swoop in and snatch people off their own property."

"Technically," he said mildly, "you were on somebody else's property."

She rolled her eyes. "Should have taken the skillet," she muttered.

And again he had to smother a chuckle. And she wasn't done yet.

"So what alphabet soup agency is it? CIA? DEA? DHS? Who spent my tax dollars for you to show up and treat me like a common criminal?"

"Rather better than, I think," he said, another little jolt hitting him as he realized he was actually *enjoying* this. He quashed the feeling as he laid the bacon into the now-hot skillet.

"Fine," she snapped. "So we're at Camp Cupcake. That's still not an answer."

"We're not government."

He was a little surprised he'd made the admission. Not that it wouldn't have a desired effect; if they were government, she might be more inclined to just cooperate. Then again, she didn't seem overly appreciative of the "alphabet soup," as she'd put it, that gurgled out of Washington, D.C. Maybe not knowing would keep her scared, and thus more cooperative. But he didn't like the idea of trying to keep her scared, effective though it might be.

As the tempting smell of sizzling bacon began to wake up his stomach—and hers, too, judging by the way she tilted her head and sniffed—he made a decision. He turned to face her. She was still holding the heavy mug of coffee, which would probably still be hot enough to do some damage if she hurled it at him. He wasn't sure he'd put it past her.

"Hayley," he said. She said nothing, but still he saw the use of her name register; he never had before. "We're not the bad guys."

She studied him for a moment before saying, "Since my life is full of clichés lately, let me add another. If it walks like a duck and quacks like a duck..."

"If I'd had any other choice, you wouldn't be here."

He saw the skin around her eyes tighten, saw her lips part, then close again, as if on words she wasn't sure she should say. That smart—and sexy—mouth....

"Everything else is 'we,'" she said.

He had to give her points for picking up on that, he guessed. "Not groupthink. My decision."

"Because you're the boss."

"I am." He saw no point in denying the obvious.

"So you're the one I should blame for all this."

His mouth quirked. "That would be me."

She wasn't short on guts, Hayley Cole wasn't, he thought,

using her full name in his mind for the first time. When they'd bought the place that was now a probably still-smoldering ruin, they had of course run full checks on all the neighbors. Rather, Charlie had; when you had one of the best on the job, it would be foolish not to use them. And when her mother had died eight months ago, it had turned up in one of Charlie's regular rechecks.

She gave a little shiver, and he wasn't sure if she was fighting to say something, or to stop herself. When she spoke, he wasn't sure if she'd won her battle or lost it.

"Why didn't you just kill me?"

This had gone far enough. Just the fact that he was enjoying this told him it had to stop.

"There's still time," he said, injecting what he hoped was the right balance of exasperation and threat into his voice. It seemed to work. At least she fell silent.

But somehow he doubted she would stay that way.

Chapter Fifteen

Hayley, we're not the bad guys....

She shivered at the memory, wrapping her arms around herself. Scary part was she wasn't sure if the shiver was born in fear, or in the edgy awareness of Quinn that had begun to torment her. And the way her name had sounded on his lips.

She groaned inwardly at that thought. The very last thing she needed was to do something stupid. And she had a perfectly good explanation for why her pulse had gone into overdrive when he'd said her name in that deep, gravel-roughened voice of his. After all, it had been a very long time since she'd even thought about a man in her life. She'd met a few, but no one had sparked any interest. Taking care of her mother had sapped the energy out of her, and she'd assumed she was still in that numbed mental state.

Until this man did nothing more than say her name.

"Stop it," she ordered herself. "You're just off balance, that's all." She should think about what he said, not how he'd said it. And certainly not how he sounded when he said her name.

...we're not the bad guys.

But bad guys would say that anyway, wouldn't they? To lull her into cooperating? They'd say anything, tell her anything. They'd play good cop, bad cop, too, wouldn't they? To get her to confide in Liam, or maybe Teague, who had to be playing good cop? There was obviously no question who the bad cop was.

Although she had to admit, those moments in the kitchen had seemed...different somehow.

Yeah, because watching a tough guy cook turns you to jelly?

She was afraid it was true. Which was why she'd retreated to the loft, instead of staying down in the great room as she had taken to doing because it was more comfortable for reading. But now she needed to think, and think clearly. She needed to analyze and decide what she was going to do. Was she going to simply go along and hope it would end well, or fight back and try to make sure it did? Would it even make a difference?

She could be a model prisoner, and they still might kill her in the end, because she could identify them. And that thought rankled; she'd rather go down fighting, if she was going to die in the end anyway. At least it would probably be quick that way.

Obviously Quinn was in charge of the day-to-day operations. And his word was law; no matter which of the others she asked questions, the response would always be the same. "Sorry, can't talk. Quinn's orders." Well, Rafer omitted the sorry. The niceties didn't seem to be in his repertoire. But the result was the same. If she wanted information, she was going to have to get it out of the boss.

At least, she was pretty sure he was the boss. Except...

All of this seemed to revolve around Vicente, and she wondered again if perhaps her former neighbor—obviously he wouldn't be going back, since the house was in ruins—was their real leader. He could be coordinating everything, but since he was holed up in the bedroom all the time, she would never know. Maybe he was the big boss, and Quinn was just following his orders.

Her mind rejected the idea; Quinn had been deferential to the older man, but not in the way of employee to boss. More in the way you were with an important customer or client.

It hit her then. Quinn *had* been deferential to Vicente, and if her gut was right, that was something he didn't do lightly. So something about Vicente, who he was or why he was here, had earned Quinn's respect.

She knew by the way her mind kicked into gear, racing to turn over and inspect all the possibilities, that she was on the right track. This whole thing revolved around the man with the silver beard. She really was incidental, an archetypal case of being in the wrong place at the wrong time. And perhaps it was Vicente who was, by his order, keeping her safe. He'd seemed concerned, in those moments before Quinn had ordered him not to speak to her, that she'd gotten swept up in this.

But Quinn had ordered him. And he had meekly obeyed. Did that mean he wasn't the leader? Or simply that in this situation, Quinn knew best? Was that even possible, a leader who could admit somebody below him had a better idea?

Just about proves they're not government, she thought wryly.

She wrestled with it all for a very long time, and reached what she thought were the only possible conclusions.

One, they were in fact bad guys, in which case she was likely dead no matter what, and it could get very, very ugly.

Two, they were good guys with no plans to kill her, in which case it wouldn't matter all that much what she did or said. If she kept pushing she'd either get locked down or... she'd get some answers.

When she coupled those two options with the simple fact that it didn't seem to be in her to go quietly along, her course of action was clear.

She might be doomed, but she'd go down fighting.

Chapter Sixteen

"Where's Vicente from? Originally, I mean."

Quinn kept chopping onion, ignoring her much as he would a gnat who was annoying but harmless. Although he would just swat away a gnat. And as much as he wanted her to go away, swatting just wasn't on the menu of options.

"I'd ask him, but of course he's not allowed to talk to me."

He was regretting offering to switch with Liam and make dinner; he'd been secretly flattered when the guy had picked up chicken on his supply run, bothered to buy ice to keep it cold all the way back, all in the hopes Quinn would make his spicy chicken with chilies fry-up. The dish was a favorite of the young Texan's, and normally Quinn didn't mind at all.

He only minded now because of that persistent gnat. This had been a very long four days, and if things didn't proceed as planned, if there were more delays, it was going to be very wearing.

"It's interesting. I've never been a pariah before."

I'm sure you haven't, thought Quinn.

She'd said it casually, with the sort of curious interest one might give…well, her dog, for one. Although Cutter went a bit beyond interesting. He'd never seen or even heard of a dog like this one. Liam had grown up in a family that bred dogs, and even he acknowledged Cutter was…different.

"Never seen a dog so smart, or who learned so fast. I mean, I had an old retriever that I used to joke could read my mind, but this dog…I'm not sure it's a joke."

Quinn knew the feeling. The second night they'd been here, he'd been ready to set out on his patrol of the perimeter and had realized he'd forgotten his trigger gloves. It was cold enough that he was about to go back to the cabin and get them when Cutter showed up at his side, as he had the night before.

Only this time, the dog had the forgotten pair of gloves held delicately in his mouth.

He glanced over to the doorway to the kitchen, where Cutter was sprawled, in the perfect position to trip up anybody trying to get in or out. But, Quinn noticed, he was angled so that he could see the front door, yet keep an eye on them in the kitchen. And he had to admit, the certainty that the dog was doing just that was an oddity.

"First time I've ever seen him really relax," he said.

Hayley's mouth twisted into a rather rueful smile. "At home he only does that when he's satisfied he's put everything to rights. Don't know what it means now."

As if on cue, the dog lifted his head to look directly at them both. And Quinn could have sworn the dog's expression was just that, satisfied, as he put his head back down and let out a sigh of relaxation.

Everything to rights? As in, he and Hayley, cornered in the same room?

He was not given to fanciful thoughts, and quashed that one immediately. It was the darn dog, he thought. He just didn't act like an ordinary dog.

"Where'd you find him?"

"I didn't. He found me."

Quinn paused in the act of slicing chilies. "What?"

She gave a half shrug. "He just turned up on my front porch

one day. That collar, and the tag with his name. I tried to find his owner, ran ads and everything, figured the weird shape of that tag would be a giveaway, but I never got any answers. I even called the coast guard."

Quinn blinked. "What?"

"The coast guard. The name Cutter, and the tag looks sort of like a boat. So I thought maybe he belonged to somebody in the guard, maybe aboard a cutter. But no luck there, either."

"So you kept him."

She looked bemused, as he often felt lately. "I didn't seem to have much choice. After a couple of months, I couldn't imagine life without him. I...needed something then."

"Needed?"

"My mother had just died a couple of weeks before."

He stopped slicing and looked at her then.

"I was feeling pretty aimless, after two years of being focused completely on taking care of her."

He didn't even realize until he heard the faint tap of wood on wood that he'd set down the knife. An odd sort of ache was building inside him, and his hand was up and moving before he realized that he was about to reach out and cup her face. He yanked it back, even as he realized there was no way to hide the quick motion. He curled his fingers, digging his nails into his palm, using the pain as distraction.

Distraction from what would turn this whole thing to pure disaster.

Distraction from what he suddenly wanted so much he didn't trust himself not to take it.

He wanted to kiss her. Long and hard and wet and deep.

He grabbed the knife again even though his brain suggested it wasn't perhaps the best idea.

"Your choice," he said sharply, once he could remember what she'd said about taking care of her dying mother.

She blinked, drew back slightly. "It was. Of course it was. I loved her. But that didn't make it any easier."

Damn, he hadn't meant to say that.

"I just meant some people don't make that choice," he muttered, almost under his breath. He went back to slicing the last chili determinedly, wondering what the hell had gotten into him.

After a moment he heard her ask softly, "You?"

He didn't answer, hoping she'd just shut up and go away. He attacked the chicken with as much determination as if it had a knife of its own and was ready to fight back.

"Did you have brothers or sisters to do the job, is that why you didn't have to care?"

"Don't you have a book to finish reading?"

The words slipped sharply from him, violating the silent vow he'd just made not to get sucked into this. Cutter's head came up. Quinn thought the dog was reacting to his tone, but the animal was looking the other way.

"Sure. But since I have all the time in the world these days…"

She said it blithely, with a careless wave of her hand. As if this were just an ordinary conversation under ordinary circumstances.

"Nobody," he snapped, "has all the time in the world."

She flinched, although it was barely perceptible and she hid it well. If he wasn't so edgy, he'd admire her nerve. Again.

"Just wondering," she said in a credibly casual tone, "why some people abandon the ones they supposedly love."

The knife slipped, cut into the pad of his left thumb. He swore, grabbing a paper towel to apply pressure and stop the bleeding.

"I was ten," he said through gritted teeth. "If anything, it was the other way around."

He'd finally managed to silence her. He should be satisfied, but instead he was utterly, thoroughly disgusted with himself. Using the grim circumstances of his life to shut up a woman who got on his nerves was not his proudest moment.

"Get the hell out of here and go back to your kids' book," he said, and it was barely a step above a snarl. He was aware the leash was slipping on his temper. And so, apparently, was

Cutter; the dog's head came up and he looked from Hayley to him with a new alertness.

"It's a kids' book, all right," she said, as if he'd said it wanting an explanation. "Full of abandonment and trials and unfairness, and eventual triumph. Perhaps that last one is why it's so enjoyable. You should try it."

"In case you haven't noticed, I have a knife in my hand."

"I noticed," she said. "I also noticed the only one bleeding at the moment is you."

He turned on her then. Stared her down with a look that had cowed armed men.

"Get. Out."

She hesitated for that fraction of a second that told him instead of instinctively running, she was actually considering what might happen if she didn't. Was she crazy? Or just too gutsy for her own good?

But then she turned and went, and he'd never been so glad to see the backside of anybody.

And all the ways that could be interpreted, fueled by appreciation for that fine backside, erupted in his imagination, and he forced himself back to shredding chicken with a ferocity that threatened to make his thumb start bleeding again.

Chapter Seventeen

Hayley managed to control her shaking until she got out of the kitchen doorway. But then she ran smack into Rafer, back from his watch and standing just a couple of feet out of sight.

"Singed?" he asked, very quietly, as if he didn't want Quinn to hear.

Hayley glanced at the older man, saw a spark of something in those dark, haunted eyes that looked oddly like admiration. Or maybe it was just interest? Curiosity? That made a lot more sense.

"Maybe a little," she admitted.

"I gotta admire your nerve, lady. He's an intimidating guy, and not many men I know would stand up to him the way you just did, pushing like that."

"Might be good for him if they did."

She wasn't sure what had made her say that, or what had possessed her to speculate what might be good for the impossible man who had her so on edge. And to one of his own men.

"Maybe. Rattle his cage a little."

This support from such an unexpected quarter startled her.

For a moment she just stared at this man who had been a quietly lethal—about that she had no doubts—presence since they'd arrived here.

"I'm not sure anyone could rattle that cage."

Rafer studied her for a long, silent moment. And finally the slightest hint of a smile curved his mouth. It was something she'd never seen before, and it struck her suddenly that, when his face wasn't grim or his eyes haunted, this was a handsome man.

"I don't know. I've known him since he was a kid, and I've never seen anybody get to him like that."

"Maybe he just doesn't like his prisoners talking back."

Rafer lifted a brow. "Prisoner?"

"What would you call it?"

"Nothing. Which is exactly what I'm going to say, as ordered. Because I want some of that fry-up of his before I head out to the perimeter."

"Too bad you can't hide from me, like Vicente."

"Be careful," came Quinn's voice from behind her, "or we'll reverse this and you can stay confined to the bedroom."

She froze. She refused to acknowledge the crazy place her mind had careened when she'd heard the word *bedroom,* even in this context, said to her by this man. Just as she refused to acknowledge the way her body tensed up in a hot, tight way any time she was close to him. She simply wouldn't, couldn't accept that she could be that stupid.

She spun around. "Why haven't you?"

"His choice."

"Why?"

"That's his business." He gestured to Rafer, a nod of his head toward the kitchen. "It's ready, and the skillet's hot. Turn the heat down after you get yours."

Rafer nodded and vanished quickly into the kitchen. Whether he was glad to escape or simply hungry for Quinn's concoction, she had no idea.

"So you've ordered all your men not to talk to me, too?"

"No."

"But he just said—"

"I've ordered them not to talk about this operation. You want to chat about the weather, wizards or anything else, have at it."

"How generous of you," she said, making no effort to rein in the sarcasm in her voice.

He studied her much as Rafer had. But for reasons she didn't want to analyze just now, it unsettled her much more.

"You just never quit, do you?"

Before she could answer, the outer door opened.

"Sorry," Liam called from the doorway. "Thought I'd see if I could borrow Cutter. I'm on my way to the south side now."

"Wait," Quinn ordered the other man. "I'll take it. Go eat."

Liam's face lit up. "Seriously?"

He didn't have to be told twice.

"Smells great," he said as he passed them. "Tastes better, huh?" he said to Hayley.

"I wouldn't know," she said, managing to tamp down the urge to sarcasm this time. It *did* smell good. Wonderful, in fact. Her stomach growled quietly on the thought.

Liam's gaze flicked from her to Quinn and back. He started to say something, then clearly thought better of it and darted into the kitchen.

"You're quite the host," she said when he was gone. "Cooking and all."

Quinn gave her a chilly look. "I'll cook for my men, my family and *invited* guests. Everybody else is on their own."

"Like I had any choice about being uninvited," she muttered.

"It is what it is," he said, sounding exasperated. "Can't you just make the best of it?"

"Make the best of it?" She stared at him. "I get kidnapped, dragged off to the back of beyond, you won't even give me a hint as to why—"

"I've told you it has nothing to do with you."

"I'm here, aren't I?" she retorted sharply. "So it has everything to do with me."

"So you're one of those women who thinks it's always all about her?"

"Oh, please, enough with the diversions," she said. "I know better than that, even if you don't."

If he was surprised that she didn't take the bait of his insult, he didn't show it. But then, until today he hadn't shown much of anything, emotion-wise at least.

I've known him since he was a kid, and I've never seen anybody get to him....

She wondered what exactly had gotten to him now; she'd asked questions before. And she'd pushed before, when he'd refused to answer those questions.

She wondered why he was so cool and remote in the first place. She wondered, stupidly, what he'd been like as that kid.

And even more stupidly, perhaps unforgivably so, she wondered if he'd reacted this time because he was as edgily aware of her as she was of him.

Under normal circumstances, in the normal world, the thought might fascinate her, even thrill her a little, a man like Quinn unwillingly reacting to her.

In these circumstances, in this crazy situation, it should terrify her.

What she was actually feeling was an unsettling combination of all those emotions, leavened with a hearty dollop of fear brought on by the fact that she still had no idea who he was, what he was doing or what this was about.

Instead of thinking about whether Quinn was as aware of her as a woman as she was him as a man, she should be worried about staying alive. She should be worried about what was going on, about the story behind the man hidden behind that closed bedroom door. She should be worried about escaping all this somehow, no matter that she had no idea where she was except that it was a long way from any outpost of real civilization.

Instead she was letting herself be lulled, convinced they really weren't bad guys, lulled by the routine the days had fallen into, fascinated by Liam's seeming boy-next-door charm, by Teague's polite, military demeanor and his thoughtfulness in picking up things for Cutter on his supply run. She was even drawn, in a way, by Rafer's haunted, sometimes pained determination.

But mostly she was captivated by the cool efficiency and rigid control—most of the time—of their boss.

Not to mention that one glance from those eyes made her heart pound. Yeah, she was the perfect prisoner, wasn't she? she thought, unleashing the full force of her sarcasm on herself. She'd never felt so tangled, so confused, so like she was going to fly apart at any moment. And Quinn walked away from her as if she didn't exist.

Without another word he grabbed up his jacket from the rack by the door, checked the weapon that he seemed to don as regularly and easily as other men put on shoes, and went outside. His absence didn't calm her much; how did she reconcile the man she kept telling herself she should be afraid of with the man who would not only cook for his men, but take the watch for one of them so he could eat?

A low whine came from Cutter as he stared after the man who had so taken his fancy. Yet he showed no sign of following, instead stayed close by her side as she walked over to the couch, as if he'd sensed her turmoil and decided his place was here this time.

As if, indeed, she thought as she sank down, feeling as weary as if she hadn't slept at all. She'd long ago given up trying to understand what uncanny instinct made the dog understand her mood so well. And she couldn't help feeling a twinge of satisfaction that the dog had chosen her over Quinn when she'd needed him to. Petty, perhaps, but there it was.

She threaded her fingers through the thick fur at his neck, trying to focus on the dog instead of the man who had just walked out, without much luck. She could read, but she who thought she could never get enough reading time was actually tired of it. She was used to doing, going, not sitting around all the time, and she was as antsy as Cutter got when his outside time was curtailed. Too bad it took more than throwing a stick to distract her.

It would, she thought glumly, take a lot more than that to get the man called Quinn out of her head.

Chapter Eighteen

"What are you guys hiding from?"

Liam gave her a sideways look as he took a bite of Quinn's concoction. Cutter, still sticking with her for the moment, sat at her feet, but watched the young man with the food hopefully. Sometimes he was just pure dog, she thought.

"What makes you think we're hiding?" Liam said after he'd swallowed.

"You didn't come here for the fine beaches and tropical breezes."

The young man grinned. "It has its own appeals."

"Like what? Lack of neighbors? Isolation? Impossibility of escape?"

"All those," Liam agreed as if that last were a normal requisite one might ask of their real estate agent. "But it's also got wide-open spaces, peace, quiet and being able to actually see millions of stars at night."

It was the stars comment that got to her. Because it was one of the things she had missed most about being in the house she'd grown up in. When she'd moved, gone to work in the city, the stars had been lost, swallowed up by the constant glow of city lights.

"Are you from a place like this?" she asked, genuinely curious. "Or is it because you're not that you like it?"

He hesitated.

"I'm not asking you to tell me *where* here is," she said. "I know you won't. Quinn's made sure of that, hasn't he?"

Liam shrugged. "Quinn's a little short in the trust department. With reason."

"Who let him down?"

She immediately regretted letting the question slip out; Liam clammed up as quickly as…well, a clam. He handed the patient Cutter the last bit of chicken, made a lame excuse and escaped to those wide-open spaces outside.

That Quinn was a little short on trust was hardly a revelation, she thought. She wondered who or what made him that way. A friend? Colleague? A woman? Or was it some longer-ago betrayal? It seemed almost silly, a man as big, as strong as Quinn being tortured by some childhood memory, but she knew it could happen.

If anything it was the other way around.

What he'd said echoed in her head, just another part of the mystery that was Quinn.

She paced the great room, as she'd taken to doing, antsy for movement, exertion of some kind. Never setting foot outside at all was beginning to wear on her. She wasn't used to doing nothing, and she was finding long, lazy days weren't as appealing as they might sound.

Of course, long, lazy days because you were being held prisoner weren't exactly a vacation.

She heard voices on the porch, and instinctively walked that way. Liam she recognized. He must have stopped on the porch. But the other voice wasn't Quinn's. She felt a jab of disappointment that annoyed her. She had to stop this, get this stupid reaction every time she saw him or heard his voice under control.

It was Rafer who stepped inside, glanced at her and nodded,

then headed for the kitchen for his own lunch. The limp was worse today, she noticed, and there had been a new tightness in his face. But he still moved quickly, even if he was in pain.

Still annoyed at herself, she retreated to the sitting area and took up her usual spot on the sofa. The book she'd been in the middle of sat on the coffee table and she picked it up, hoping the story would distract her from her inward irritation. At least it would keep her from feeling she had to make conversation with the closemouthed Rafer.

Cutter leaped up beside her. With his usual uncanny intuition, the dog seemed to know she needed his steadying presence at the moment.

After a couple of minutes Rafer appeared with a sandwich and a glass balanced in one hand. *Gotta keep that gun hand free in case the little woman jumps you,* she thought sourly. She knew it wasn't fair, really, they all did it so automatically she knew it probably had little to do with her. They'd been trained, well trained, and it was likely as second nature as waking at any sound in the night had become to her when she was taking care of her mother.

Rafer sat down on one of the chairs opposite the big coffee table and began to eat his lunch, rather methodically she thought. As if it were as impersonal as simply taking in fuel. Almost as if he were irritated at having to do it.

She tried to focus on her book; obviously the man was in no mood to talk. A few minutes later, after she'd heard the sound of the glass being set down on the table, Cutter slipped quietly off the couch. He made no sound on the rug, so after a moment she looked up to see where he'd gone.

To her surprise he was sitting at the gruff man's feet, watching as he rubbed at his left leg just above the knee. Was it pain that made him seem so prickly all the time? Pain that put that scowl on his face, that tightness around his mouth?

Cutter moved then, swiping his tongue over Rafer's left hand. The man's head jerked, startled, and he froze as he looked at the dog with a stunned expression.

With an audible sigh, Cutter leaned to rest his head against the spot Rafer had been rubbing, as if he could ease the pain. Hayley knew from personal experience that, with her at least, the dog had exactly that effect. It was no doubt simply distraction from the ache, but however it worked, she couldn't deny it did. But Rafer Crawford wasn't exactly the kind of guy she'd expect to believe that.

But even as she thought it, the man lifted a hand. Slowly he lifted one hand, and with a tremor Hayley was sure he'd have hidden if he realized she was watching, laid it on the dog's head. Cutter's tongue swept out again, laying a doggy kiss across the fingers of the hand that had been working the sore spot.

Rafer wore the strangest expression she thought she'd ever seen on a man. A confused mix of wonder, wariness and welcome. That he could feel such a tangle of emotions over a simple expression of aid and comfort from a dog spoke volumes about where this man lived in his head.

She quickly turned her eyes back to her book; the last thing she wanted was to get caught watching what somehow seemed a very private moment. A betrayal of emotions she was sure he'd rather keep hidden, at the least.

She sensed rather than saw him get up, heard him pick up the dishes. Only when he turned and began to walk toward the kitchen did she risk a look. After about three steps he slowed. Reached down to touch his leg. Then took three more steps.

He stopped. His head snapped around. For a long moment he stared at the dog, his brows furrowed.

Hayley went hastily back to her book, her question answered. She hadn't needed to see his face to know that the pain had eased, she'd known by the improvement of his limp. Cutter had worked his small miracle again.

Amazing how he always sensed who needed that particular kind of attention. When she got back home—if she *did* get back home—she was going to have to look into therapy-dog training. She might not be able to explain how he did it, but he had the knack for making anyone sick or injured feel better. She would do it, she thought, suddenly determined.

And it wouldn't be some empty promise made to some higher power, to be forgotten once she was safe again. The dog had some sort of canine genius, and if it could really help people, it should be put to use.

The dog returned to his spot on the couch beside her. He curled up and rested his chin on her leg. She reached to scratch his right ear in that spot he loved. He sighed happily.

He even made her feel better about this situation, she thought. Or maybe just less alone. Less scared. Something. It was probably as simple as the desperate hope that the dog's uncanny judgment hadn't failed, that when he'd decided so instantly that he adored Quinn, it wasn't some aberration.

And again she was back to the same two basic conclusions. Either the dog was right, they weren't bad guys but, despite their actions, worthy of his help and in Quinn's case, adoration and respect. Or he was wrong, they were bad guys, and she wasn't going home. Ever.

Cutter would be fine either way, she thought. They'd found him useful, would probably take him with them when they were done here; she'd heard Liam and Teague both talking to Quinn about the feasibility of adding a dog to their team. Why not one who'd already proven himself as helpful? He'd need some training, probably—training that would be far different from the therapy-dog training she'd been thinking about.

She shivered slightly, despite the warmth of the room. Quietly, rationally considering what would happen after your own imminent demise did that to you, she guessed.

...we're not the bad guys.

"I hope you're right, furry one," she whispered to the dog.

Cutter lifted his head, and swept that soothing pink tongue over her fingers. She went back to her book, reassured.

She only wished she could hang on to that feeling the next time Quinn was the one who came through that door.

Chapter Nineteen

The inactivity was making her twitchy, and Hayley was teetering on the edge of volunteering for kitchen duty. She supposed she should be thankful they hadn't assigned it to her, hadn't assumed she *should* do it because she was the sole woman.

Maybe that meant more than she'd realized. She'd been pushing back, slowly, against Quinn's order that she stick to the loft and the bathroom, and so far last night had been the only incident. She'd come back downstairs late, needing that bathroom. And had found Quinn and Vicente sitting at the small eating bar that separated the kitchen from the main room, talking. Intently. In Spanish.

He didn't even look at her, but held up a hand to stop Vicente, then switched to English and said, "Make it quick."

"It'll take what it takes," she snapped.

To her surprise, she thought she saw Vicente smile, albeit guardedly.

"Chica valiente," he said, so softly she barely heard. Not

that it mattered, her Spanish was limited to the ever useful *"Habla Ingles?"*

Quinn had said something in return, and while she had no idea what it meant, there was no mistaking his wry, almost irritated tone.

She could have looked it up, she thought now, if she had her smartphone—assuming she could get a signal here—or if she had access to that laptop of theirs, but that was clearly out of the question. She shuddered to think what her email inbox must look like by now.

Which made her wonder anew what was going on in the world she'd left behind. Her kindly neighbor Mrs. Peters would wonder where she was, at least, but enough to report her missing? Probably not. Hayley had spoken to her, musing idly, about taking a trip, getting away for a while. It seemed inviting, a good way to decide what she wanted to do with the rest of her life, although she'd made no concrete plans. Mrs. Peters might well assume she had done just that, even though it would be very odd for Hayley to do so without letting her know.

She'd quit her job to take care of her mother, and thanks to the nice inheritance that was now hers, she didn't need to go back to work unless she wanted to—and frankly, she hadn't missed her work in the county clerk's office all that much anyway. But now there was no one to miss her when she didn't show up at an office or something.

Her best friend, Amy, would be getting worried, she knew. They spoke or emailed every couple of days, and had plans to get together at the end of the month when Amy had vacation coming from her job as a paralegal down in L.A. She'd be more likely to make a fuss, Hayley thought. And Amy was a force to be reckoned with, when she got motivated. She—

"Hayley?"

She snapped out of her reverie with a start as Liam said her name. She realized he'd been standing there for a moment, and was now looking at her curiously. No wonder, she'd been so lost in her own thoughts she hadn't even been aware he was there. At least not consciously; subconsciously she must have been, because she suddenly realized what he'd initially said to her.

"Outside?"

"Quinn thought you might be getting a little stir-crazy. So if you want to go for a walk, now's the time."

"This is Quinn's idea?"

She didn't know which astonished her more, that he'd agreed to this, or that he'd had the idea in the first place.

Liam chuckled. "I know he comes off as scary, but really, he's a good guy."

Hayley wanted to believe that. For her own sake. "Then why won't he talk to me?"

Liam's expression changed, his voice taking on a tone of almost-amazed amusement. "Now that's interesting. Teague thinks he's annoyed you're even here. Rafer thinks it's because you get to him, and he doesn't like that."

That answer set up an immediate battle in Hayley's mind. No matter how much her common sense, her logic, her sense of self-preservation told her the next question should be either "Why am I here?" or "Where *is* here?", the question she most wanted to ask was "What do you mean I get to him?"

Don't be an idiot female, she ordered herself.

"Which do you believe?"

"I have to choose?" Liam said, with an exaggerated look of dismay that would have amused her under any other circumstances.

"I'm not here by choice," she reminded him, rather sharply.

"I know. And I'm sorry about that. We all are. We know how scary it must be."

She thought of the team, of the four tough-looking, well-trained men. "Somehow I doubt that."

"No, really."

"Right. You know darn well any one of you would probably have escaped by now."

"Look, Hayley, we're not—" He stopped, clearly frustrated.

"The bad guys? So I've been told. Then why can't I get some simple answers?"

"Orders."

"Quinn's orders?"

"Yes."

"And Quinn's orders are sacrosanct, is that it?"

"Pretty much, yeah."

Liam didn't look the least bit discomfited at admitting it. Was his admiration that complete, that he wouldn't—or couldn't—ever question? Blind obedience?

"To just you, or—"

"To all of us. To anybody who works with him."

Which implied, she thought, that there were more than just these three men in that category. How many were there? And where were they?

"Why?" she asked bluntly.

Liam looked at her steadily for a long moment. It was hard to believe there was any ill intent behind those innocent-looking, soft brown eyes.

"Because he's the boss. He built this operation. Because he pays my salary, a good one. Because he gave me a chance at something better. But most of all, because he's earned it."

"You talk about him like he's some kind of—"

"Don't let her get to you, Liam."

Quinn's voice came from behind them; he'd come in so quietly neither of them had heard him. At least she hadn't. She wasn't sure Liam hadn't known it, and hence the high praise, intended to be overheard.

"Get back out there. Rafer saw a dust cloud in an odd place a minute ago. Nothing since, but I want the extra eyes out."

Liam nodded, but flicked a glance at her.

"I'll deal with this," Quinn said, and the younger man turned on his heel and exited like someone escaping a coming storm.

This? The word and his tone had hit a nerve already raw, depersonalizing her, sounded as if she were merely some bug to be swatted or, worse, dishes to be done.

"No, thanks," she said, rather fiercely. "I'd rather stay inside than go for a walk with *you.*"

"You're not going for any walk. You wasted your time asking questions you knew weren't going to get answered."

She hadn't realized how much she'd wanted to go out until he'd yanked the opportunity out from under her. "What?" she yelped. "It was only what, five minutes?"

"Better than nothing, which is what you have now."

"Don't treat me like some kid you have to teach a lesson to."

"Just a law of nature. Despite those who would like to deny it, actions have consequences."

"And reactions," Hayley muttered, wishing she was the sort of woman to deliver a roundhouse slap to that hard-jawed face of his. But somehow she doubted that, even if she got her full strength behind it, it would have much effect.

"Equal and opposite?" he said, with that vague amusement that irked her.

"Opposite, anyway." She met his gaze, figuring she had nothing to lose. "What is it you're afraid will happen if you tell me the truth? It's not like I can run next door and tell someone."

"Not unless you're up to running sixty or so miles in this heat."

"Then what's the point of keeping me in the dark, if you're really not the bad guys?"

"It's for your own good."

Being treated like a child was one thing, being talked to like one on top of it was the last tug on Hayley's already stress-aggravated temper.

"And just what the hell makes you think you have any right to decide what's good for me?"

"I ended up with that right when you poked your nose where it didn't belong."

"I didn't poke my nose anywhere, my *dog* did! And you sure don't seem averse to letting *him* play your little game."

Quinn went very still. "This is no game," he said, his voice flat, and more grim than any she'd ever heard except for the doctor who'd told her her mother was dying.

"Isn't it? Isn't it all, with your helicopter and your guns, a big, deadly game?"

"Nothing involving guns is a game," Quinn said. "At least it shouldn't be."

The unexpected and uncharacteristic bitterness of his last words surprised her. She wondered what he was thinking of, what had brought on the comment.

"Do you shoot?" he asked.

"I've shot skeet, a few times." Her mouth twisted. "Not handguns. My mom hated them."

"Hating guns isn't going to help you out here."

"I don't hate guns, they're only tools. My dad was a cop. They can save lives, fight evil. And take lives and perpetrate evil. So I just hate them in the wrong hands."

"Well, well. Something we can agree on." When she didn't speak his mouth quirked. "Obviously you don't think we're the right hands."

"How could I know?" she asked, not bothering to hide her sarcasm. "It's not like your name's all over that fancy helicopter."

"I object to that description," he said. "It's powerful, efficient, sleek and altogether cool, but fancy it's not."

Altogether cool...?

For a moment she just stared at him. He'd sounded like a boy with a new, heart's-desire toy. And for an instant, he looked like one, too.

"Whose is it?"

"Mine," he said with a satisfaction that matched that look.

"Yours? Not your boss's?"

"I don't have a boss. Well, except Charlie." His mouth quirked again, wryly this time. "We all answer to Charlie."

Instinctively, she nearly smiled at his tone. She caught herself in surprise. But she couldn't deny that at some time during this conversation that had started out so heated, something had changed. There was something so normal about his voice, his expression, now. Not a softening, she doubted if this man could ever be called anything remotely resembling soft. But a change nevertheless, a change that made him...less intimidating, less menacing somehow.

She was about to ask who Charlie was when he asked a question of his own.

"Your dad was a cop?"

She hesitated, wondering if she should have let that slip out. If she'd been thinking instead of angry, she might have considered if it was wise to let them know that before she came out with it. With any of the other guys, she probably would have; if they weren't good guys, then knowing she was in any way connected to a cop might tip them over into doing something about her.

But thinking seemed to fall by the wayside with this man. Besides, it wasn't as if she could unsay it.

"Yes," she said.

"Was, as in is no longer?"

"Was, as in killed in the line of duty when I was sixteen."

Something changed yet again in his face. The hard-edged planes, the strong jaw didn't shift, but his eyes widened just slightly, and his lips parted as if for breath, or words.

"I'm sorry," he said.

The words were simple, timeworn, and oft-heard, but never, she thought, had they sounded more sincere.

"Me, too," she said. "It's rough. Losing a parent so young."

She remembered again what he'd said, about being the one abandoned when he was ten. And she would swear there was a sad knowledge in his eyes, beyond the words that she'd heard so often they'd descended into platitude. Why could she suddenly read him so easily, when usually she found it impossible to even begin to guess what he was thinking? Was it because he was letting her see past the mask?

Or was this a new mask, donned to gain her confidence, her trust, and through that, her cooperation?

She didn't believe it. The remembered pain in his eyes was too clear, too real, too overwhelming. If that was faked, then she might as well give up and let them kill her, because she was too stupid to live.

"Quinn," she began, then stopped, in part because she'd never said it before and it felt strange, in part because she wasn't sure what she wanted to say anyway, and in part because of the way he went still when she said it.

She wondered if he would say her name back, but he didn't. He just looked at her. And it was with some certainty that she asked, "Who was it for you? Mom? Dad?"

"Both," he said, his voice so inflectionless she knew it was intentional, and she wondered what the neutrality cost him. When she'd thought about some childhood betrayal, she'd never thought of this.

Both his parents. At ten. That was more horrible than she could imagine. Losing her dad had been bad enough, but to lose both of them, at an even younger age—

Cutter's trumpeting bark from outside cut off her grim imaginings. Quinn's head snapped around.

"That's a warning bark," Hayley said, then felt silly for explaining the obvious.

Quinn was already crossing swiftly to the window. Hayley got there just in time to see Cutter streaking out of sight past the barn, head down, tail out straight; whoever it was was going to get a doggie greeting the polar opposite of what Quinn had gotten.

Quinn yanked the handheld radio from where it was clipped on his belt, forgoing the usual earwig since he was inside. "Report!"

"I heard, but the southeast perimeter's clear," Teague's voice came back.

"Half way around southwest, ditto so far." That was Liam, she recognized the trace of the drawl even over the radio.

"Rafer? I think the dog was headed your way."

"Hang on, heading for higher ground."

Quinn said nothing, but he didn't simply wait. He crossed to the gun rack on the far wall, unlocked it and took out a weapon that looked aggressive and menacing by its very design; unrelieved black like the helicopter, with an odd shape and all kinds of scopelike gear attached.

"Dog's cued on something to the northeast, I'm almost to where—"

Rafer's voice broke off, nearly stopping Hayley's heart. She'd come to like the guy, she realized.

"I've got incoming hostiles," Rafer's voice came over the small radio, so quietly that it made his words even more unsettling. "At least six on my front. Mile, mile and a half out. On foot, well armed."

For an instant Hayley just stood there, stunned. All of a sudden this was no longer an irritating and frightening puzzle. This was a war. A very small but very real war.

And they were under attack.

Chapter Twenty

Quinn snapped orders, not because his men didn't already know what to do, but to remind everybody where the friendlies would be. Each man had long ago scouted his sector and chosen his high ground; Teague in the dilapidated-looking windmill, Liam in the hayloft of the barn, with its panoramic view, and Rafer, as usual, in the farthest, most dangerous, most exposed spot, the single place that could really be called a hill in this mostly flat place, and the first line of defense. That the man was a sniper of the highest class made that line of defense more than formidable.

"I've got 'em. Still nearly a mile out," Teague said over the radio, and Quinn acknowledged, knowing from the background sounds that the man was getting into position already.

"Four more. Same distance."

Rafer's voice was, as always in these situations, deadly calm.

So ten men at least. "Any chance they're IBs, local hunters or hikers?"

Rafer didn't laugh at the idea they were innocent bystanders, but his answer was so swift he might as well have.

"Not unless they do a lot of hunting around here with high explosives. One guy's draped like a suicide bomber."

Quinn's jaw tightened at the familiar phrase. He calculated quickly. Each observation location had been fitted with a cache of handy weapons, including some explosives of their own. Not just out of expectation they'd have to use them, but because preparation was the best way to ensure they wouldn't.

Was there enough? He smiled inwardly; of course there was. Charlie would have seen to it. There'd be enough ordinance here to fend off a small army. Maybe even a big one.

Teague's voice crackled. "You want the chopper?"

"Not yet," Quinn said. "Until we see how they're armed. Don't want fly into an RPG or a Stinger or something."

The last time they'd run into a group like this, rocket-propelled grenades had not only been on the menu, but the surface-to-air missiles, as well. He had to keep the aircraft in reserve in case they had to fly Vicente out of here. Once he was safe, and only if all else failed, would the helicopter be outfitted with its nice little .50 caliber and used as a weapon. All they had to do was get it armed and airborne, and any remaining opposition could be cut to shreds.

But it was their job now to make sure it didn't come to that. And their job alone; if the operation had been compromised, which seemed likely given how fast they'd been found again, they couldn't risk breaking silence to call in more backup. He'd been right to stay dark, but it gave him no satisfaction. What it gave him was another job to do; find the mole, as soon as this was over.

He was making his own preparations, slipping on a vest and filling the many pockets with various things. To he himself fell the task of being the last line of defense. He'd rather be out there, stopping this before it got started, but Vicente was still their top priority, and it had to stay that way.

Even if a smart-mouthed, quick-witted woman had complicated matters immeasurably.

"Who are they?" Hayley asked as he went back to the gun case and began to select other weapons, a luxury he might not have had if not for Cutter's early warning.

"That dog of yours," he said, "is a help. Nice to have warning."

"Yes. Who are they?"

"You said you went trap shooting. You any good?"

"Better than fair, not expert."

"That'll do," Quinn said, turning back to the rack of long guns, selecting one, a Mossberg 500. "It has the extended magazine, seven plus one." He handed it to her, with a box of shells. "Load it, and you can have it."

She took it without hesitation. He had to hope she'd shoot the same way if it came to that. She fed the shells in with only a slight clumsiness, as if she knew perfectly well what to do, but hadn't done it in a while. After a moment of assuring himself she really did know what she was doing, he went back to his own task.

He picked up two of the small grenades and slipped them into the vest's large left pocket. And after a moment's hesitation, he picked up what looked like an industrial-strength stun gun. He turned to face her.

"You ever use one of these?"

She barely glanced at the electronic weapon before shaking her head.

"It's fairly basic," he said. "Make contact, push button."

She made no comment on the instruction. "Who are they?" she asked for a fourth time. And for a fourth time he ignored the question.

"The shotgun's a good weapon, but keep this handy just in case. If they get this far, my job is to protect Vicente. You'll be on your own."

If this announcement of her lack of importance in the overall scheme of things shocked or bothered her, it didn't show. He had to give her credit, she didn't rattle easy.

"Who are they?"

"They," he finally said, with no small amount of exasperation at her stubbornness, "are the bad guys you've been worried about."

All the while he was thinking. Two groups, one small, one larger. Where would the leader be? These were civilians, not military, so ordinary command structure didn't apply. It would depend on his orders and his ego, Quinn thought. If he was the type who needed that ego fed, he might be with the larger group, needing the feel of being in charge of more people.

If it were him, he'd be with the smaller, more maneuverable group. And that group would be made up of the best they had, be it shooters or bombers or hand-to-hand experts. The big group would, by its size, draw the most attention, allowing the smaller group to get closer.

He keyed the mic. "Anybody tell if they've got the head?"

"Got a guy gesturing a lot," Teague answered.

"Cool and quiet lot," Rafer said.

That decided Quinn. The guy doing all the waving likely thought of himself as the leader, maybe even had the title. But the other, smaller group could be the bigger threat; cool and quiet indicated experience, professionalism or training.

"Attack assessment?" he asked.

"Looks like straight ahead," Liam said.

"Ditto," Teague said. "They're making some effort to stay hidden, but I don't think they realize how far you can see out here."

City boys? Quinn wondered. "So we have two fronts confirmed?" he said into the handheld.

He got two responses in agreement, then a pause. He waited for the assessment that would mean the most.

"My gut says three."

The certainty in Rafer's voice came through the small speaker. And if Rafe was certain, Quinn knew better than to doubt him; the man's gut was as legendary as his sniper skills.

"Direction?"

"It was me, I'd come in over the mesa behind the house while we're fighting head-on."

Exactly what he'd do if he were trying to take this place. If it were true, they weren't dealing with complete amateurs.

"Want me to change position?" Liam asked; he was the only one who apparently had an empty field of fire in front of him.

Quinn turned to look at Hayley. "Can you set that dog to guarding something specific?"

She frowned. "Yes, but—"

"Hold your location, Liam, you've got the best view of the mesa from up there," Quinn said, ignoring whatever her "but" would have been. "Who's got the dog?"

"He just left me," Rafer said.

"Headed for me," Teague said. "I can see his tail."

"See if you can send him back here."

"And just how do I do that? You know what they say about giving somebody else's dog orders."

"Tell him to find Hayley," Quinn said.

"He'd probably have better luck," Hayley said, her tone sour, "if he told him to find Quinn."

Quinn flicked a glance at her. By her expression, he guessed that his amusement was beginning to irritate her.

"Jealous?"

"Just trying to figure out a usually reliable dog who's lost his ability to judge good character."

She had said the words before, but the heat in her voice was gone now. Quinn turned then, to face her straight on. She was looking up at him, her face so readable to him, the fear, the doubt, the annoyance, it was all there, so clearly. There was even hope there. It had to be hope that he hadn't lied when he'd told her they weren't the bad guys, he thought.

And underneath it all, buried by that tangle of emotions, was something else, something he'd been trying desperately not to acknowledge. Some hyperalertness in the way she looked at him, and in the way her gaze shifted over him in the quick, darting way of someone making sure they were really seeing what they thought they were seeing.

The same way he caught himself too often looking at her.

"He hasn't lost it," he said quietly.

For an instant she didn't react, and he wondered but didn't dare speculate where her mind had wandered. But then she clearly remembered her own words about Cutter's judgment. Her eyes widened slightly, the barest stretching of the muscles of expression.

And then the sound of racing paws sounded across the wooden porch. Cutter was here.

Quinn opened the door and let the dog in. For once the uncannily smart animal ignored him and went straight to Hayley. Teague had told him to find her, and find her he had. He sniffed her up and down, nudging her hand with his nose, not settling until she patted his head, assuring him she was fine. As if he'd understood, the moment she said the word "fine" the dog spun around to look at Quinn. Questioningly, for all the world like one of his team awaiting orders.

He was definitely going to have to think about adding a canine to this team. Although he wasn't sure dogs like Cutter came along often.

"Can you help me guard the back, boy?"

Quinn knew he wasn't imagining the change that came over the dog at the word *guard*. The tail-wagging stopped, the ears stopped swiveling and focused—if that was the word—on him. Every line of the dog's square, lithe body drew up, suddenly tensed and ready. His dark eyes were fastened on Quinn's face, and so intense that for a moment he understood how those hapless sheep felt.

And then, in the next moment, Cutter blew Quinn's expectations and everything he assumed about dogs in general to pieces. He pivoted on his hind paws and headed for the back of the cabin.

Quinn stared after him. That the dog understood the word "guard" was no surprise, really. He supposed many dogs did. But "back"? How had he understood that?

His gaze flicked to Hayley. "How did he know that? How did he even know what I meant by 'the back'?"

"He knew."

"Obviously. But how did he know I didn't mean my back, or yours, or the back of just this room?"

"Because he's Cutter. He's not…" She hesitated, then continued. "He's not just a dog. Not an ordinary one, anyway. Sometimes I think he's a bit…"

Again she trailed off. Quinn knew he needed to get moving, but somehow this answer seemed crucial. "A bit what?" he prompted.

"Magical. Fey, at least."

The whimsy was unexpected, silly even, but she said it so hesitantly he knew she knew how it sounded.

And now was certainly not the time to have a discussion about potential supernatural qualities of a dog who was no doubt simply very, very smart.

"I've got range."

Rafer's voice crackled over the radio. Quinn thought quickly. If Rafer said he had range, that meant that group was down to two, maybe one as soon as he gave the order. The man simply didn't miss. Teague wasn't quite as good at that distance, but he could take out one for sure, maybe two of his larger group.

But once shots were fired, the force that was counting on surprise would know they were no surprise at all. So what would they do, learning they'd lost that advantage?

Depends on what that knowledge costs them, Quinn thought.

It was up to them to make that knowledge very, very expensive.

He headed for the back of the cabin.

Chapter Twenty-One

Hayley's heart was hammering in her chest, and she tried to breath deeper, slower. Her brain, however, wasn't racing. It was stuck in a silly, stupid rut as she watched man and dog meld into an efficient working team. As he always had with her, the dog seemed to respond not just to what Quinn said, but sometimes even before he said it. It was as if they'd been together for years.

Quinn stopped at the door of the bedroom, calling Vicente's name. And for only about the third time since they'd been here, Hayley saw her neighbor step out of the bedroom where he'd retreated for seemingly the duration.

"We have been found?" he asked.

"Looks that way." Then Quinn did something that once more shook her entire perception of everything that had happened; he handed the man one of the deadly looking pistols he held. "You know these men even better than I do. If they get this far, use it."

Vicente took it, handling it with familiarity, she noticed. "But...you will not let that happen?"

"If they get to you," Quinn said flatly, "I'll be dead."

Hayley's breath caught anew in her throat.

"And this will all have been for nothing," Vicente said sadly. "The murderers will go unpunished, and my head will make the journey back to my home, to be displayed on a post as a warning."

Hayley's breath caught. Murderers? The men after him were murderers? Quinn said nothing. Vicente glanced at her. She stared back. His head? As in, beheaded? She gave herself a mental shake, willing her brain to start functioning again.

"And an innocent woman will die, as well." Vicente was looking at Hayley with a sadness that made her feel, for a moment, bad for the man, even though it was obviously her own death he was prematurely regretting. Then the stark reality of it all began to set in, and fear kicked through her. She'd been better off, she thought, when her brain had been numb.

"I should have listened to you, written it all out," Vicente said.

The memory of what she'd overheard the other day flashed through her mind. She didn't know what Quinn had wanted Vicente to write out, but she knew now he'd wanted him to do it because he'd foreseen this possibility. Then the man had naturally been focused on his own well-being, but now he was obviously realizing Quinn may have been right.

She had the feeling Quinn was often right, at least about such things as this.

"Just keep the gun with you and ready."

The radio crackled. "They're closing in on my position," Teague said. "Less than a half mile now."

"Copy," Quinn snapped. "Hold for a couple more. Liam?"

"Thought I saw a bit of dust kicked up on top of the mesa, but there's a bit of wind, could be nothing."

"Assume it's not," Quinn ordered.

"Copy that."

Quinn turned back to Vicente. "If anybody gets through, it won't be many. Two, maybe three at most. I can promise you that."

"These are ruthless killers," Vicente warned. "Your men are that good?"

"They are," Quinn said.

He turned then, clearly intent on finishing his preparations. Cutter, obviously on high alert, paced near the back door while Quinn moved equipment from the weapons locker to various places in the cabin. It took her a moment to realize he was placing the items so they would be at hand if he had to retreat through the house from the back.

In a few moments he appeared to be satisfied, and headed toward the back of the house. And Cutter.

"What are you doing?" she asked as he reached for the lever-style handle on the door.

He glanced over his shoulder at her. "What I told Liam. Assuming that dust wasn't just the wind."

"You're not going out there?"

She hadn't meant to yelp, but it came out that way anyway. He just kept going.

"Let me amend that," she snapped. "You're not taking my dog out there."

He stopped. Turned. "What would Cutter do if someone threatened you?"

"He'd protect me, get between me and them," she admitted. She'd seen it, that day a drunk had stumbled out of the restaurant next to the post office right into her, and Cutter had done exactly that. That he had failed to get between her and Quinn was an anomaly she wasn't thinking about at the moment.

"That's what he's doing. Just a little earlier."

"But these men have guns."

"Yes. So do we."

She couldn't help glancing at Vicente; her quiet former neighbor hardly seemed like the gun-wielding type. Yet he was handling the weapon with an easy familiarity.

"Oh, he can shoot," Quinn said, with a grim undertone in his voice that hadn't been there before. "If they get in here, both of you get into the bedroom. Vicente, you know what to do."

The man nodded. Oddly, Hayley thought, he didn't look frightened, only regretful.

"What good will that do?" she asked.

"The room's armored, and there's a special lock."

Hayley barely had time to absorb that.

"Now or never!" Rafer's voice crackled over the radio.

"Time to start this party," Quinn said. The grimness, oddly, was gone from his voice. It took Hayley a moment to realize it had been replaced with…not excitement, or exhilaration, but some kind of adrenaline-pushed energy. Men at war, she thought inanely.

"Rafe, take out who you can. Other positions, hold and watch their reactions. When you see what they've got, what they do, respond appropriately."

Whatever appropriately means, Hayley thought, not able to think much past if they shoot, shoot back. Obviously the men knew, because no questions crackled back over the radio.

The reality of it just wouldn't sink in. That men were likely going to die here, in the next few minutes. Maybe even one of the men she'd come to know. Liam with his drawl, Teague with his charming smile, Rafer with his slower, more precious smile. Or even Quinn, standing as the last barrier between those men and what they wanted.

She shivered involuntarily. Not at the thought of Quinn going down, not any more than anyone else, anyway, she told herself. It was simply that the idea of gunfire tearing into this remote, isolated, extremely quiet place that had been her home for days now seemed utterly unimaginable, it was too—

As if her own thoughts had brought it on she heard three shots in succession. Big, loud shots. Then a rapid volley of several from two different directions, on top of each other so she couldn't tell what came from where.

"Three down, two terminally."

Rafer's voice was impossibly calm as it came through the small speaker. He'd taken out three of the four men who'd been approaching him, and announced it as calmly as he would say he'd picked up apples at the store. And she suddenly realized their job, those three men out there, was to whittle down the odds for Quinn. Her stomach knotted.

Another transmission came over the radio, Teague's voice, but Hayley missed what he said. Cutter's trumpeting, booming warning bark drowned it out. The dog was clawing at the back door, looking back at them, begging them to let him out.

They were coming.

"I'm counting on him to tell me exactly where they are. Then I'll send him back," Quinn said to her.

"But—"

"Don't argue. No time."

He started quickly down the hallway toward the dog. Hayley followed, unable to really think of doing anything else.

"But what—"

He cut her off again, this time with his hand on the dancingly eager Cutter's collar. "I'll look out for him as best I can. I don't think they'll do anything to him, since it's obvious we already know they're here."

"My question was what are *you* going to do?"

For a split second he gave her a startled look. "My job," he said simply.

And his job was to go out there alone, maybe die?

She walked to him, unable to stop herself. He was reaching for the handle of the back door. Cutter went still, his nose jammed up against where the door would open. Quinn elbowed the handle down and, oddly it seemed at that moment, she heard the small click as it opened. For an instant he looked at her.

"He'll be back shortly," he said. She wasn't at all sure the dog would desert him out there, even if ordered, but before she could speak he took her breath away yet again by pressing his lips to her forehead and adding softly, "Stay safe, Hayley."

Something in his voice made the words he'd said to Vicente flash through her mind.

If they get to you, I'll be dead....

And then they were gone.

Chapter Twenty-Two

More gunfire came from the front, rapid fire that could be anyone, and the slower, inexorable crack that was Rafer's M24. But it sounded as though he'd shifted position, and Quinn smiled, the barest hint of a smile, in satisfaction. Rafer had taken care of his first group, and was now helping Teague whittle away at his, at a distance that would seem impossible to anyone who hadn't seen the Hathcock trophy at Camp Perry, where the name Rafer Crawford appeared three years in succession as the best marksman the marines had.

He was amazed that the dog wasn't going berserk, with all these hostile strangers approaching from all directions. Yet the dog seemed to understand that their mission was here, on the back side, in these few feet between the back of the cabin and the base of the bluff.

At one time it had been the perfect protection, a near-vertical, rocky, nearly impossible drop. But over the years parts of it had crumbled, slipping down and accumulating into a slightly milder slope at the bottom. As a result, the bottom section was easier to traverse. But it was also loose, and thus more treacherous underfoot. And for his purposes, also conveniently noisy; it was hard to travel more than a few yards without knocking something loose that rattled down the slope.

Cutter was trotting along the base of that toed-out slope, his head up, tail out straight, looking for all the world like a dog on a mission. Quinn watched as he himself worked his way slowly west.

Cutter stopped suddenly.

The slightest of breezes cooled his skin, and Quinn wondered what scents it had brought the alert animal. The dog took several steps up the crumbling slope, then stopped staring upward, stock-still. For the briefest second the dog's ears swiveled back, and Quinn guessed he was making sure the somewhat-slow-on-the-uptake human was properly reading his signals.

"I got you, boy," Quinn whispered as he edged quietly nearer. He wasn't sure just how keen the dog's hearing was, hadn't really said it expecting the dog to hear, but the ears swiveled back. And all the while his nose was working, his sides going in and out like a bellows, searching, sorting.

It wasn't the spot he'd expected. This was in plain view of the cabin, once they came over the edge.

"Wish you could tell me how many," he said as he got to the dog's position.

The dog's head moved back and forth, describing a short arc that, up top, would include a distance of perhaps ten feet. Oddly, it was similar to the hand signal they used to indicate the danger zone, the spread of the enemy, how much ground they needed to focus on. If it was one of his men, the movement would indicate a small team, two, maybe three.

But it wasn't. It was Cutter. A dog. But still, it seemed—

And it also seems you're going crazy, he told himself sternly. Trust the dog's nose and ears, but don't go making him any more than just a dog.

"Seven down."

Teague's voice came through the radio earwig he'd put in his ear the moment he'd stepped outside; no sense in letting the enemy overhear your every move, not to mention shouting your own position.

"Copy," he said quietly, knowing the hypersensitive mic would pick it up. Not as good as Cutter's ears, but close.

"In back?" Liam asked.

"Affirmative. Two, maybe three."

And that was based on the sound, or lack of, he told himself. Not a chance movement by a dog. A very, very smart dog, but still just a dog nevertheless.

"Copy."

There was no suggestion one of them come to help, nor did he expect—or want—it. The day he couldn't deal with a mere two or three hostiles, he should hang it up.

The day you can't handle a woman and a dog...

Teague's joke flashed through his head. He pushed the thought away, but not before he wondered if that day had come.

Cutter moved, three steps farther up the hill, every line of his body taut as he stared upward, at the lip of the bluff. Again Quinn thought that this wasn't the spot he would have chosen, were he the attacker. If it were him, he'd take the downward slope on the other side of the outcropping just ahead, because it offered a small amount of visual shelter from anyone watching from the cabin. But he also would have waited for nightfall. So did that mean they weren't as good as he was giving them credit for, or that they were impatient?

His mouth twisted. Maybe there were enough of them they weren't worried about stealth, which also meant they had that most dangerous of outlooks, that of "acceptable losses."

Or maybe he should quit trusting a dog quite so much, he thought wryly.

But Cutter had never let them down. Since he'd been here, he'd been tireless, and never given false warning. There was always some cause, if not armed men like today, then a hungry coyote or a venomous snake, or some other threat. He knew they all had come to trust the animal's sharper senses, that was only logical. It was interpreting his signals that was tricky. He was, after all, only a dog. Even if Hayley thought he might be a magical one.

He felt a split-second flash of longing, sadness for having lost the ability for whimsical thinking so very long ago. He quashed it with the ease of long years of practice; but Hayley's image remained. He should be thinking about the operation, the job at hand, and the goal that was so imperative. Hayley was secondary, he told himself. If it came to a choice between the two, his job was to keep Vicente safe and alive. Not Hayley.

Just formulating the thought made him recoil. And for the first time he admitted to himself how much she'd gotten to him. How much he admired her courage, never giving up in what had to be a terrifying situation for her, never backing down from him, when he'd tried so hard to intimidate her. And her smarts; after the initial shock, she'd never stopped thinking, planning, but she'd also never lost sight of reality. When the impossibility of escape had sunk in, she'd wisely abandoned the idea, and seemingly resigned herself to staying put. But still, she'd never stopped pushing, gnawing at him, poking him for answers he wouldn't give.

Cutter was still frozen, staring upward. Quinn studied the striking black-and-brown dog for a moment longer, thinking of another of Hayley's qualities: loyalty. She'd literally charged at armed men to retrieve this wayward pup. He was sure she saw nothing strange in that.

I'm responsible for him. He trusts me to take care of him. It's part of the deal.

Her words came back to him, her voice ringing in his head as if she were standing right here. That he remembered what she'd said, her voice, and her face so clearly, down to the last detail of how she'd raised her eyebrows in emphasis of what she thought the self-evidence of her declaration, rattled him. He was a trained observer, used to cataloging every detail that might be helpful, so it wasn't that.

It was that in her case, those details caused a ridiculous yet undeniable reaction in him.

And made him an idiot, he thought sharply, standing here

mooning around when you've got an armed team about to descend. He had to decide, and now. This faction of the small force could crest the bluff at any moment.

Cutter was still intently focused upward in the same spot. He'd never wavered since that small breeze had brought him whatever scent had convinced him. Animals could triangulate much better than humans, he knew, with their moveable ears. But did that mean he should go against his own logic and training, which told him the spot to watch was on the other side of that outcropping?

He never was sure what made him decide. He only knew that when he moved, he was heading for that outcropping not to wait for an attack, but to use it for cover. If it could shelter men coming down the bluff, it could also hide him from men coming down somewhere else.

Like the spot Cutter insisted on.

For an instant the dog seemed ready to protest.

"It's all right, boy. I believe you," he whispered as he moved past the animal. "That's where they are. We'll turn it on them. Use the cover they should have used."

As if he'd understood every word, Cutter abandoned his post and followed. Trotting ahead until he was just past the outcropping, the dog angled up slightly and, amazingly, stopped in exactly the spot Quinn had chosen. He spun back and waited expectantly, now watching Quinn as intently as he had the top of the bluff.

Quinn shook his head wonderingly as he joined the dog. And when he turned and looked back, it suddenly hit him. From here, the profile of the slope was much clearer. And what it told him was worth volumes.

In the spot Cutter had warned him they were approaching, the slope was much gentler. More of the bluff had crumbled, making a wider toe, stretching up higher, enabling someone to come down at perhaps a forty-five-degree angle most of the way instead of sixty or seventy.

They'd chosen not the most covert way, the way most likely to guarantee surprise. They'd chosen the easiest way. Or at the least, the fastest way. And the choice told him what he needed to know.

He crouched out of sight behind the rocks, in a curved space hollowed out by the wind over eons of time. It undercut the slope above, and eventually would crumble like the rest, but for now it was solid and holding.

Cutter pressed up against him, refocused upward now.

"You're something, you know that, dog?" he whispered.

The animal's dark eyes fastened on him for a moment, and just for a moment something seemed to stir there, some quick and ethereal connection between man and beast. And then Quinn nearly gaped as the dog's expressive face relaxed into what could only be described as a grin. A doggie grin, to be sure, but that didn't lessen the impact.

Quinn laughed inwardly at himself. He'd never been prone to fantasy. The gene, if he'd ever had it, had been knocked out of him at age ten by a fierce, bloody, evil reality, and it had never recovered.

But then, he'd never been prone to obsessing about a woman he barely knew, and that under the worst circumstances, either. For that matter, he'd never been prone to obsessing about any woman, even under the best circumstances. He—

Cutter nipped his hand.

He nearly jumped, and looked down at the dog, who was back focused upward. As if the nip had been a sharp reminder to pay attention.

One he'd needed, Quinn admitted ruefully. But how the hell had the dog known—

They were here. He heard the string of sounds as a small, dislodged rock tumbled down the slope. It was an ordinary sound, one you might not even connect to a presence, or even hear if you were inside the cabin. But Quinn knew what it meant.

"You'd better get back now," he told Cutter. "Go to Hayley."

The dog glanced at the cabin, as if he'd understood perfectly. But he never budged.

"Cutter, go. Find Hayley."

A low whine issued from the dog's throat, but still he didn't move. And then a rope unraveled down the bluff and they were out of time. Hayley was going to hate him if anything happened to that dog. He wasn't sure he wouldn't hate himself. Crazy how an animal and a stubborn, nervy woman had worked their way into being so damned important so damned fast.

With an effort larger than he'd been used to making for a long time, he made himself focus before he completely lost control of the situation. Still in the shelter of the rocky outcrop, he watched their approach.

The rope had large knots every few feet, so these were no experts. Quinn knew his best chance would be when they had both hands on the rope. Which they would, unless they had harnesses that would allow them to come down one-handed, but if they had those, there wouldn't be knots.

One man came over. His hesitation at the top told Quinn he was right about their unfamiliarity with the process. They may have found them, but they hadn't prepared in advance for the mission. Not the way he would have or Charlie would have. If it was Charlie, they'd have an elevator built by now.

He hoped he lived to thank their logistical genius once more for thinking of everything.

He hoped he lived to keep Vicente alive.

He hoped he lived to keep Hayley safe.

He wondered when he'd let the word *hope* back into his vocabulary.

Chapter Twenty-Three

The shotgun felt familiar in her hands. It was a moment before she realized why her fingers were so tight around it, why her eyes were stinging. The feel of it brought her father so close, the memory of him hovering over her, directing her on how to track the hurtling piece of clay, when to fire, what she'd done wrong when she missed, or right when she hit.

She felt the urge to retreat, to go hide in that protected room now. She resisted it. Quinn was putting himself in mortal danger, putting himself between them and those dangerous men. It might well be his job, but that didn't negate the magnitude of what he was doing. So how could she simply retreat, when she was armed with a weapon she knew how to use and that was effective in a last-ditch fight, if it came to that?

She couldn't. She'd had more than enough of just sitting, waiting. She'd run through her store of patience and standing by. Instead she edged over to the small window Quinn had looked through before opening the back door. Startled, she jerked back, then looked again.

The window wasn't just glass, it was some sort of lens, like a wide angle or a fish eye, giving a much more expansive view of the area than you'd expect from such a small opening. She could see everything behind the cabin, from left to right, from the ground to a strip of sky above the top of the bluff. Whoever had outfitted this place, probably the Charlie she kept hearing about, was indeed the genius they proclaimed.

She spotted Cutter quickly, standing at the base of the bluff just before an odd vertical ridge of rock, staring upward. Quinn, for all his size, was harder to pick out in the slightly distorted image, because of the way his tan clothes blended against the matching backdrop and the fact that he was on just the other side of that vertical ridge.

Cutter moved then, over to where Quinn was, whether at a command or not she couldn't tell. She had little doubt the dog would follow a command from Quinn; he'd been astonishingly receptive to the man's every wish since he'd laid eyes on him. She didn't understand it. The dog was friendly enough with anyone he didn't take an instinctive dislike to, but he had, until now, obeyed only her. He might, occasionally, do something someone else asked, but it was usually something he wanted to do himself anyway. He'd fetch for Mrs. Peters's nephew for as long as the boy could throw, but he wouldn't do tricks for him.

But he would for Quinn. Somehow she was sure of that. The dog had just about taken out an ad declaring his devotion. And he had that annoying way of looking at her expectantly, as if wondering why she wasn't following suit, when it was so clear to him this was how it should be.

She shook her head sharply, telling herself to stop imagining a dog was thinking more than any dog thought, and pay attention. In the same moment, startling her, Cutter reached out and nipped at Quinn's hand.

Quinn jumped as if startled out a reverie. Which seemed impossible; the man never lost focus, any more than the dog did. He—

A movement from the top of the bluff interrupted her thought. Quinn's instincts had obviously been right. Her hands tightened around the shotgun. She resisted the urge to double-check the load; she knew the string of shells were there, she'd put them in herself. And she had another full load of shells in each pocket of the vest Quinn had given her to wear. If she needed more than that, she was going to die anyway.

"You should come back to the safe room."

Vicente's voice came from a few feet behind her. "Not yet," she said, not turning her face away from the slightly distorted view.

"But if they get past him—"

"I don't think they will."

"You have great faith."

She glanced at the man, realizing what he said was, at least in part, true. "In that, yes."

"But you do not trust him in other ways. In the ways a woman must trust her man."

Her man? Not likely. "Quinn," she said flatly, "is no woman's man."

"Not yet."

Vicente said it in a tone tinged with amusement and an odd sort of satisfaction. In a tone that irked her. The man seemed to realize it, because he smiled, a smile that matched the irritatingly amused voice.

"A woman needs a good man."

She turned her head to stare him down. "And what," she said, her voice as cool as she could make it, "makes you think he is one?"

"If you cannot tell that, then you are not as clever as I think you are. Perhaps not even as clever as you think you are."

A quick retort leaped to her lips, but a movement caught by the corner of her eye drew her sharply back to the window.

They were coming over the cliff.

In that instant, the last of her mind's stubborn resistance to this whole idea, the last of her normalcy bias, the idea that what was happening wasn't really happening, and that if she just waited, things would get back to normal, vanished.

It was happening. She was in a remote cabin with armed men attacking.

Knotted ropes unrolled down the bluff.

They were attacking *now*.

And she realized with a disgust aimed solely at herself that she'd been dwelling on the wrong questions all along. She shouldn't have been focused on who Quinn and his men were, or who the oncoming force was. She should have been pushing to learn who this man looking at her now was, because she realized now, too late, that that answer would hold all the others.

"This is my fault," he said, his tone regretful now. "But I assure you, I was attempting to do the right thing, the good thing."

It was too late to speculate what that would be, there was only time now to react, to deal with the threat. And hope she was alive to unravel the truth afterward.

To hope that Quinn was alive, to find out the truth of who he was.

It was the last esoteric thought she had time for. A third rope followed the first two. Men came over the edge, heading down quickly, if without much grace. They were armed, heavily, weapons in holsters and shoved into belts and larger ones slung over their shoulders. Again her grip on the shotgun tightened and she wondered if she'd lost her touch, if she'd even be able to get off two or three shots as quickly as she used to.

Not to mention that while hitting a flying clay pigeon might be trickier than a man right in front of you, the mental aspect was something else again. Although she guessed the intellectual trappings would vanish when that man was coming at you with every intent to kill.

She heard two shots.

Two men fell the last twenty feet to the ground.

Cutter barked, a loud, thunderous bark, as if announcing the start of the battle.

The third man had let go and dropped, rolling and stumbling through the loose scrabble at the bottom of the slope. She watched what happened through the fish-eye seeming window, as if it were on a distorted-around-the-edges television screen. The third man fired a blast of automatic fire at Quinn's cover, bits of rock flying in all directions. Cutter barked, angrily. She could see him, at the foot of the wedge of rock that was giving Quinn cover.

Cutter. The dog didn't know what shooting meant, did he? He tended to face threats head-on, and had no idea about guns or bullets. He might run out into the line of fire, not realizing—

Even as she thought it, she saw Quinn reach out, lay a hand on the dog's neck, pulling him back to a safer position. For an instant, Quinn's head and neck were exposed, open for a shot, and Hayley's breath caught.

But apparently no one on the approaching force was quick enough to take advantage, and she breathed again as both man and dog were back in the semiprotected position.

He'd risked his life to pull Cutter back to relative safety.

In the instant that registered, three things happened. Cutter spun around to the east, behind them, barking furiously again. Quinn, busy with the man closing in, glanced over his shoulder. And Hayley saw another man, already on the ground and coming up on them from behind. Fast.

Cutter leaped into a run. Quinn whirled. The new threat fired a burst from the same kind of automatic weapon they all seemed to be carrying. But the man was distracted by the dog and the shot went wild. Cutter was on him, a furious whirl of fur and teeth and ferocity. Hayley held her breath yet again, waiting for Quinn to simply shoot, praying that he wouldn't hit the dog and not seeing how he couldn't.

But Quinn didn't shoot. He leaped, much like Cutter had, and the whirl of man and gun and dog seemed to engulf him, too.

Another shot rang out. From the direction of the original attack. She made her decision as quickly as it had all happened. She undid the lock and pushed down on the handle and swung open the door at the same time. She heard Vicente shout, but the words didn't register. She might have lost her edge as far as hitting a small, quick-moving target, but she could at least keep that other man pinned down.

Three quick blasts from the Mossberg did exactly that, stopped the man heading for the house while Quinn was fighting for his life, stopped him in his tracks. She heard a yell, thought she might actually have hit him with a pellet or two, although that hadn't really been her goal. She just wanted him to stay put and not shoot.

Her man edged forward. She waited until she could see his leg from the knee down, then sent a shell toward his foot. He jerked backward, swearing as the small storm of pebbles and dust exploded in front of him.

A quick look told her Quinn was back on his feet, standing over the man who had come down behind him. He glanced at her; if he was shocked at her intervention it didn't show. Nothing did. He was already moving. He looked at Cutter, said something, and the dog raced toward her. Quinn motioned at her to get back inside. He looked almost angry at her.

"You're welcome," she muttered, then grimaced at her own idiocy. She reached down to gratefully touch Cutter's warm fur, and receive a swipe of his tongue in return. At least she could get the dog inside and safe. Quinn had enough to think about, with the surviving men still armed and ready.

Or maybe not so ready; they were climbing back up the ropes, rather gracelessly. For a moment, they were wide-open targets, unable to shoot back with both hands on the ropes as they scrambled upward.

And then Quinn was there, beside her, lifting his rifle, but firing only one round as the survivors vanished over the top of the bluff.

"Gone," she said in relief.

"They'll be back," Quinn said, with a certainty that rattled her.

She watched, feeling rather numb, as Quinn called out to Vicente, who announced he was fine. Liam, Teague and Rafer checked in on the radio, advising the remnants of their own forces were also in retreat. And then he knelt beside Cutter, running his hands over the animal.

"You're okay?" he said, softly. "Good boy."

Cutter wriggled in the kind of adoration she'd only ever seen before directed at her. She stared at the dog, but once assured he was all right, she wasn't really seeing him.

A shiver went through her as Quinn left her side to check the men who were down. Now that the immediate threat was over and her adrenaline began to ebb, the reality of what had happened here struck hard. Men had died here. And Quinn, the man she'd almost convinced herself was sincere, was one of the good guys, had killed three of them practically right in front of her. One apparently with his bare hands, and without sustaining any more than a small cut on his cheek.

And yet all she could think of was the reason he'd had to do it that way, in a hand-to-hand battle that had been terrifying to watch.

He'd done it because he didn't want to shoot. And there was only one reason for that. He hadn't wanted to accidentally hit Cutter.

He'd risked serious injury, or even death—although Vicente was right, she had a great deal of faith in Quinn coming out on top in any battle—rather than risk the life of a dog that wasn't even his.

And that told her more about Quinn than all his sharp comments, strict orders, or cool glances altogether.

Chapter Twenty-Four

"They will not give up," Vicente warned.

The quietly spoken words, full of conviction, made Hayley shiver.

"I know," Quinn agreed. "Rafer, long-range recon."

The man nodded without speaking, and quietly left the room, the lethal-looking sniper rifle still slung over his shoulder, and making his slight limp a very moot point.

In the lull after the fight, they'd all gathered in the cabin for this strategy meeting, which seemed to consist of Quinn snapping orders.

"Teague, check the bird, make sure it didn't sustain any damage." The former marine echoed Rafer's move and left without speaking. Quinn turned to Liam. "Get the package ready to fly."

He glanced at Vicente then, who looked grim but relieved. And apparently touched by none of the shock that was slowing her reactions, her movement, even her thinking. She shook her head sharply, trying to clear it.

"You ready to give that written statement?" Quinn asked.

Vicente sighed. "I am."

"Good. Liam, as soon as you're airborne, fire up that laptop of yours and take some dictation."

"My mom always said I'd make somebody a good secretary," the young man said with a grin.

Hayley couldn't believe he could be so lighthearted after what had just happened here. Again she shook her head, nothing was making sense, although everybody else was acting as if things were perfectly clear.

"We'll get you out of here safely, sir," Liam said to Vicente. "Trust us."

"You have proven yourself willing to die to protect me," Vicente said, his tone the only one matching how she was feeling inside. "I trust you."

Belatedly, it occurred to her to wonder what was going to happen to her, now. Would she be evacuated along with...whatever he was?

Protection.

Written statement.

If I do what you ask, they who want it will have no need of me.

Vicente's words rang in her head, and suddenly the answer seemed so clear she knew she should have seen it before.

They *were* protecting Vicente. Because of what he would say in that statement. The statement somebody very much wanted.

He was a witness. To something. Something big.

Her only excuse was that protected witnesses were not something she came across in her quiet life. And she would have also assumed protecting a witness was the government's job. But still, it all fit so perfectly she knew she should have seen it before. Long before.

And that it definitely and safely put Quinn and his team on the side of the angels didn't hurt any.

But why weren't those angels protecting their own?

She shook her head a third time, although she didn't expect it to do any more good than it had before.

"Adrenaline crash," Quinn said.

Hayley blinked. "What?"

"Adrenaline lets you function under stress, but it also depletes you. Drains you. That's why you're shaky, and your head feels fuzzy, like you haven't slept for a week."

That's exactly what it felt like, so she took his words seriously. She fastened her gaze on him. Saw he was looking at her steadily, as if assessing her. He'd done that before, in fact almost constantly, but there was something different about it now. Something different about the way he was looking at her, something different in his eyes.

Something softer.

"That was a nice bit of work you did out there, Hayley. Thank you."

An anger she couldn't quite explain sparked through her. "So that's what it takes to get you to treat me like a human being? Almost killing another human being? And watching you kill three, plus one with your bare hands?"

For a moment the room was so silent she could hear the ticking of the military-style, twenty-four-hour clock on the wall. Her angry words seemed to echo, bouncing around until they sounded harsh even to her. Hadn't she just decided he really was one of the good guys? And he had risked his life, gone up against seven men alone—well, he and Cutter—to do it. She might have helped, but not much.

And the fact that the goal had been to protect Vicente didn't change the fact that he'd saved her, too. He had put himself in the line of fire with full intent and knowledge, and here she was, snapping at him.

"The crash also saps your governors," he said quietly. "makes you lash out, do and say things you wouldn't if you weren't so drained."

She was feeling like an idiot now. "But you're completely calm."

"I've learned to control it, over the years. The adrenaline surge, and the crash." He very nearly smiled at her. She was almost glad he'd stopped himself. She wasn't sure she could withstand that. Instead he quietly restated what'd he'd said before.

"You did good out there. You shouldn't have done it, mind you, and I should be chewing you out for stepping outside when I told you to stay safe, but once you did, you did good."

She stared at him. "Well, if that isn't the most backhanded, double-sided, damned-with-faint-praise compliment I've ever heard."

The smile came then, leaving Hayley breathless, and with the unmistakable impression that she'd just played right into his hands.

"Now that's the Hayley we've come to know and love," Liam quipped.

She realized suddenly that the jitters had stopped. The trembling she'd noticed, like shivers from a nonexistent cold, had ebbed. And she knew with a sudden certainty that had been Quinn's aim. He'd gently jabbed at her to get her to think about something other than what she'd just witnessed.

And she also noticed that at Liam's words, Quinn's expression had changed again, softened even more. It was an infinitesimal shift around his eyes and mouth, but it had happened. Either he wasn't hiding as well, or she was learning to read him. She wasn't sure how to feel about either option.

"Bird's good, boss."

Teague's voice crackled over the radio. Quinn spoke into the mic on his shirt collar. "Give it another twenty, to full dark, then fire her up."

"Copy."

Full dark. She'd been so wrapped up in what had happened she hadn't even realized how close they were to darkness.

"That's how much time you have," Quinn said to Vicente, who merely nodded and turned to walk back to the bedroom, Liam on his heels.

He shifted his attention back to Hayley. "You, too."

"Good thing I have nothing to pack," she said, thankful she'd kept up on the laundry, alternating her own clothes with the sweats and T-shirt from the cabin's stock. She was in her own now, so she didn't even have to change.

Once more he stood there, assessing her. She held his gaze, glad her voice had been relatively steady.

And then, slowly, Quinn smiled at her. And unlike the first time, there was no ulterior motive, no jab to jolt her out of the shivering aftermath of the adrenaline rush. Just a genuine smile.

"You'll do, Hayley Cole. You'll do."

For an instant she thought she should be offended; who was he to make that judgment? But reality forestalled her; he was the man who obviously knew what they were facing and how to deal with it.

Belatedly it struck her just how ruthless the men after Vicente must be. They were willing to kill four men, an innocent bystander and a dog to get to him. And sacrifice several of their own to do it.

And Quinn was convinced they hadn't quit, they'd merely retreated to regroup for another attack. He hadn't been wrong yet.

It was the fastest twenty minutes of her life. In the moment she realized the light had faded, she heard the distinctive sound of the helicopter's engine starting up. Moments later Vicente and Liam emerged from the back of the cabin, Liam with the older man's duffel over his shoulder.

"I'll get the go bags," Quinn said. "You—" He stopped suddenly, one hand snapping to his ear, indicating he was listening. Liam obviously heard the same thing, because instantly he began to hustle Vicente toward the door.

"Get back here, Rafer. The bird's live." Quinn turned to her. "Let's go. They're on the move. We've got only minutes."

She didn't waste time arguing, not after what she'd seen today. "Cutter," she called, sharply enough that the dog, who had been pacing restlessly, knew she meant business. He was at her heels in seconds.

By the time she got outside, Quinn at her elbow, Cutter sticking close, Vicente and Liam were already aboard. Hayley's heart leaped when she saw a figure approaching from the west, but calmed again when she recognized Rafer's slightly impaired but seemingly unslowed run. By the time Quinn had helped her and Cutter aboard, he was there.

Rafer glanced inside the helicopter, lingering for a moment on Teague, at the controls. Then he looked back at Quinn.

"Why'd you call me back?"

"Get on board."

Rafer shook his head. "You know we're pushing the limit as it is."

"Get on board."

"We'll never make it with all of us."

"I know. Get on board."

"Somebody needs to lay down cover—"

"I know. Get on board."

"Boss—"

"Do it. My decision."

As Rafer complied with obvious reluctance, Quinn shifted his own gaze to Teague and raised his voice to be heard. "Head north until you're over the horizon. Then get the package— and the civilian—to location Z. Do what you have to do. Once you're clear, contact Charlie. No reason not to now, they've already found us."

Teague nodded. She was obviously the civilian, she guessed, but location Z? Hayley's mouth quirked; that was a corny name if ever she'd heard one. She was a little surprised she could even muster that much reaction, after everything—

It hit her then.

We'll never make it with all of us.

Somebody needs to lay down cover—

I know.

Rafer's argument suddenly made sense. Quinn was going to stay behind. He'd ordered Teague to take off, and leave him behind. *Lay down cover.* He was going to stall them, hold them off until they were clear.

"Quinn, no!"

The words broke from her involuntarily. Quinn's gaze

shifted. And he gave her that smile again, that smile that changed everything.

"Stay safe, Hayley."

As he said those words to her for the second time, she wondered for an instant if that was what he always said when he headed into a situation he didn't expect to come out of.

It was crazy. He knew that, he had to know that, it would be just him against all the men who were left. He was good, she couldn't doubt that after what she'd seen, but they'd be looking for blood, revenge. They'd already proved they were ruthless. She had no doubts anymore that Vicente's story of his head making the trip home without him was nothing less than the truth.

But Quinn was going to make sure they got away safely.

No matter the cost.

Even if it was his life.

Chapter Twenty-Five

The rotors began to turn as Teague focused on preparing for takeoff. In desperation Hayley looked at Rafer, who was seated in the copilot's seat now. He returned her gaze, letting the full knowledge of what was happening show in his eyes.

"He'd have my head if I didn't follow his orders."

"So instead they get his?"

Rafer looked surprised, then bemusement spread across his usually expressionless face. Followed by an unexpected smile she didn't understand.

Her head snapped back to Quinn, who was loading Vicente's duffel behind the second seat. Before she could speak he stepped back and reached for the helicopter's door as the pitch of the engine changed, escalated to full power, making any further conversation impossible.

Teague made the final adjustments she now recognized. She could still see Quinn through the narrowing gap as the door began to slide shut.

Cutter gave a sharp yelp. He was looking at Quinn as well,

and apparently realizing the object of his adoration was not coming with them.

The dog exploded into frenzied motion, startling Hayley and breaking free. He leaped to the ground beside Quinn. He looked back at Hayley, barking urgently, audible even above the helicopter's engine. Instinctively, without thought, as had become habit, she moved to retrieve her dog.

The door nearly caught her as it slid shut. She hastily stepped down to the skid, and the door latched behind her. She gasped as she saw the gap between the helicopter's skid and the ground, realized they were already lifting off.

She had no choice, she was already in motion and knew she would fall if she tried to stop. Better to jump, and have some control.

It was only a three-foot drop, but it seemed like more when she hit ground. She wobbled for a moment as one foot hit a rock and slid, but then Quinn was there, his strong arm steadying her even as he swore, words she hadn't heard since the time her father had found her hiding in Toby Baxter's tree house, hours after a fight with her mother. He'd been terrified for her; Quinn, she was sure, was just angry.

He made a circular hand gesture toward the helicopter. It didn't take much to guess what it meant; keep going. Hayley had never thought she'd be sorry to see the last of that black helicopter, but the reality of the situation began to sink in as the aircraft lifted out of reach.

She didn't have time to dwell on feelings of abandonment. In the moment that Quinn grabbed her arm and starting pulling her back toward the house, she heard odd popping sounds. She thought something had gone wrong with the helicopter, but it continued to rise, began to assume the angle she knew now meant they were about to start making speed.

Quinn whipped up the rifle he held. Fired bursts of automatic fire to the west. She barely stifled a startled yelp at the sound. The helicopter kept rising. Quinn pushed her to the ground behind him. He went into a crouch, rifle still up. Little puffs of dust and pebbles kicked up from the dirt within inches of them.

Gunshots. What she had heard before were gunshots, she finally realized. They were back.

Quinn sent out another spray of fire, apparently knowing where the shots were coming from. Cutter stood beside him, barking angrily, as if he understood the threat. Who knows, Hayley thought numbly, maybe the uncannily smart dog had learned the danger of gunfire during that last heated battle.

Quinn grabbed something out of his vest. He rose slightly. Her mind screamed "No, they'll see you!" in the instant before his arm came back and he threw. Cutter jumped forward a little, wire-drawn and frighteningly intent. She grabbed the dog's collar. She didn't think even the sometimes amazingly strong Cutter could drag her deadweight with him. Not that that would stop him from trying.

The explosion was deafening, even to ears still ringing from the sound of gunfire. The grenades, she thought, a little numbly, also belatedly realizing they had probably known exactly where he was from his return fire anyway.

Quinn fired again and again, and she couldn't even see who he was shooting at. But obviously he could, and since the helicopter seemed safely out of range now, he had clearly succeeded with his goal of covering their escape.

He threw another grenade.

And then she had no time to think at all; Quinn had her running. Another grenade exploded. She felt the shock through the ground, swore she could feel it rock the very air around her. But they kept going, so fast all she could think about was staying on her feet as he charted a dodging, crooked, crazy path back toward the cabin.

Then they were inside, and Quinn slammed and secured the door behind them. She wasn't sure what good it would do stopping bullets, but she hadn't known about the armored bedroom, either.

Quinn whirled on her.

"Not many people do something that stupid and survive," he snapped.

"I know," she admitted, and saw the surprise in his eyes at the ease of her capitulation. "But it was too late to stop. And I couldn't just leave him."

Quinn glanced at Cutter. The dog looked from him back to her, and Hayley could have sworn there was a look of approval—even satisfaction—in his eyes.

"I can see why sheep obey him," she murmured.

"Are you saying he made you do it, or that you're a sheep?" Quinn asked. She wished there had been a bit more humor in the question.

"Maybe both," she said, suddenly weary.

For a moment Quinn said nothing. When he did speak, his conciliatory tone—and his words—surprised her. "He does have a way."

"Yes. Yes, he does. And a powerful will."

"Must be how it works. The sheep."

She didn't know if it was supposed to be another jab at her, but she felt the need to explain. "He does do it with people, too. I don't know how, he just communicates."

Quinn nodded. "I've seen it."

She felt a little relieved, his anger seemed to have ebbed.

"I could do without the smugness, though," Quinn said.

Hayley's gaze shot to his face; had that been a joke? But he was looking at the dog, a wry expression on his face. Could he really see it? Usually it was only she who read such human emotions into Cutter's expressions, and she kept the notion to herself.

"He does seem a bit full of himself," she said carefully.

"He looks," Quinn said drily, "like a guy whose plan has come together."

Hayley's eyes widened. She never would have expected something so…fanciful from the cool, commanding and undeniably deadly man before her.

"Make yourself useful, dog," he said to Cutter. "Let me

know if they decide to make another run. Guard," he added, making a sweeping gesture around the cabin.

The dog gave a low, whuffing sound, she supposed the canine equivalent of "Yes, sir," and trotted off toward the front door and the single window. He began to pace, stopping now and then with his head cocked, clearly listening, or with his nose up, sniffing deeply.

"I swear, sometimes I think he's…" Quinn's words trailed off.

"Me, too," Hayley agreed. "Sometimes I really wonder. And then he chews up a shoe, or digs a huge hole in the yard, or brings me a dead rat, and I realize he's just a dog again."

"At least he'll be a help." Just like that, that softer Quinn vanished, and the professional was back. And none too happy with her.

"Unlike me?"

He looked at her then. "You held them off with that shotgun, even if you did miss."

"I didn't miss. I wasn't aiming *at* them."

Quinn drew back slightly. "Are you saying you could have hit them, but you didn't?"

"I didn't want to kill anybody—"

"There is a time for mercy," Quinn said, his voice suddenly like ice. "When the men trying to kill *you* don't know the meaning of the word is not it."

He didn't point out that her qualms had left them with more men to deal with now, and for that she was grateful.

"You'd better believe this now, Hayley. Those men out there are beyond ruthless. They are the kind of men who kill for revenge, to make a point, to teach a lesson and simply because they enjoy it. And your innocence will not protect you. You are in their way, and that's all it takes."

"But so many of them have died—"

"They're as ruthless with their own as they are their enemies. They'll keep coming to the last man. My team will come back with help, but until then we're on our own. And we, in case you hadn't noticed, are pinned down here."

She felt shaken, but she couldn't deny the truth of what he'd said, she'd seen it for herself. She drew in a deep, steadying breath, and let it out in a quick gust. She walked to table where she'd dropped the shotgun when she'd come back inside. She picked up the powerful, reliable weapon and methodically re-loaded it.

Then she turned to face Quinn.

"What else can I do?" she asked, working to keep her voice calm, although inside she was scared to death.

He looked at her, assessingly. His gaze flicked to the shot-gun, then back to her face. He gave her a short, sharp nod of approval, and she was stunned at how good it made her feel.

"We may need to retreat to the armored room. Move any food that doesn't require cooking in there. There's also a cache of freeze-dried food in the closet."

She nodded. "What about water?"

"There's a tap in there. And bottles we filled when we first got here."

"Somebody thought of everything," she said.

"Charlie," he said, already moving before she began to walk toward the kitchen. He was rechecking all the places where he'd left weapons earlier. Then he started carrying what was left in the weapons locker into the bedroom.

By the time she was done, the locker was mostly empty, everything that wasn't out and within reach of various parts of the room was moved into the safe room.

Including all but one of the boxes of shells for her shotgun.

"What if I need more?" she asked, eying the box.

"If you need more than that," he said, "you'll be heading in there." He gestured toward the bedroom. "Shotgun's best at shorter range. If they get close, your job is to just keep them back until you can get into that room and lock it."

"You say that like I'll be alone."

Even as she spoke she already knew the answer. He'd given it to Vicente, barely an hour ago.

If they get to you, I'll be dead.

Chapter Twenty-Six

She was holding up remarkably well, considering.

Quinn made another circuit, checking the carefully placed windows. As with everything else here at this site and all their others, Charlie had sited them personally, at the best possible observation points. And before long Vicente would be tucked away at their most impenetrable and unassailable stronghold, one rarely used for various reasons, but in this case he'd not hesitated to give the order.

One of those reasons was at this moment in the kitchen, and his nose had just told him why; the enticing aroma of fresh coffee had wafted his way.

Good thinking, he told her silently. But then he'd come to know she was good at that. She never stopped thinking.

Except for that moment when she'd come after her blessed dog. Again. He'd intended for her—and Cutter, for that matter—to be out of here and safe before the next attack.

And yet he, the cool, unemotional pragmatist, understood. And that surprised him. But Cutter was an amazing dog. Like now, for instance; instead of being at Quinn's heels, he was on the opposite side of the cabin, obviously alert and on guard, nose twitching, ears swiveling. And every time Quinn moved to another viewing post, Cutter moved in turn, so at least two sides of the cabin were always covered.

In other words, Quinn thought in amazement, the dog was doing exactly what he would have ordered one of his men to do. Oh, he wouldn't have picked those particular places, but the animal apparently knew what spots gave him the best audio or olfactory reception. Amazing indeed.

Hayley approached him with a mug of hot coffee.

"Thanks for thinking of this," he said, accepting it and taking a sip. It was exactly as he liked it. Obviously she'd seen him do it enough times to get it just right.

"Don't know if there'll be a chance later," she said.

Her voice was low, quiet, and he didn't miss the undercurrent of strain. He would have been amazed if she was calm, indeed would have assumed she didn't understand the severity of their situation. But she obviously did.

"They'll be coming back soon," he said between sips.

"Why didn't they just keep coming now?"

"We were in the open, now we're not. Their first plan of attack here didn't work, now they need a new one. And it's getting dark."

"You think they won't come in the dark?"

"No idea. Depends how desperate they are."

He took another gulp of coffee then set the mug down. There was no point in sugarcoating this for her. And it seemed she was able to handle reality better than most in her position would be, so he gave it to her.

"If they have enough ammo, they may just open fire and try to tear the place down with bullets. If that happens, you run for the bedroom."

"And leave you out here to do...what?"

"My job."

"I thought your job just left on that helicopter."

Like I said, she never stops thinking, Quinn thought wryly.

"And you should have, too."

"I don't think we have the time to waste going over that again."

He couldn't stop his mouth from quirking upward. "Point taken," he said.

He glanced at the items he'd selected from the weapons locker. As soon as it was fully dark, he'd go out and set some booby traps. There were some land mines which, if put in the right place, could give the illusion of an entire minefield. Trip wires, portable laser beams that sent up a shrieking alarm, he had many options.

And he might be using them all tonight.

"Who are you? Who's Vicente, really?"

He hesitated. Her chin came up. She stared him down in a way few men had the nerve to do.

"If I'm going to die out here because of all this," she said, "I damned well want to know why."

"You're not going to—"

"You can't guarantee that. They found us here, didn't they?"

She had a point, and one he couldn't deny. A couple of points, actually.

He chose to give her the answer that would come out eventually anyway.

"Vicente Reynosa is going to be the prize witness in hearings about a drug cartel that's murdered hundreds, maybe thousands of people along the Mexican border. Including nearly two dozen American citizens."

Her eyes widened. "The man they've been talking about on the news?"

He should have guessed she'd probably heard the blaring news reports about the investigation. Hard to miss, given the fury over how long, and how many deaths it had taken to get the bureaucracy moving. Vicente was the only person they'd found willing to give evidence against the huge, well-armed and utterly ruthless cartel.

"He's...a drug dealer?" She sounded astonished.

"Not really. He was coerced. Forced to cooperate with the drug lord. They hold his family. His wife, three children and his sister. They've already tortured and brutally murdered his only son."

He saw the expressions cross her face, and found them as readable as if she'd spoken every stage, from shock, to the realization that her neighbor was in fact a hero of sorts, to anger.

"Those bastards," she exclaimed.

"Exactly."

"And good for Vicente. No wonder you respect him."

"Yes. He's a brave man."

"What about his family, when he testifies?"

"We're working on that." He gave her a sideways look. "If it makes you feel any better, the guy I killed with my bare hands, as you said? He was the one who tortured and murdered Vicente's son."

He saw something spark in her green eyes, a flash of satisfaction that warmed him. It was a moment before she said, "Which brings me back to my other question."

No, she never stopped. He let out a compressed breath.

"Hayley," he began.

"Are you government agents?"

"No."

"But I thought that's who protected witnesses."

"Normally, it is."

"But?"

He opened his mouth to say something diverting, one of the usual answers given to anyone who got too curious. But what she'd said before stopped him cold.

If I'm going to die out here because of all this, I damned well want to know why.

It was a very grim, very real possibility. When he coupled that with how she'd handled all this, keeping what had to be extraordinary fear under control, and dragging up enough courage to not only confront him at every turn, snipe at him, argue with him, but when the chips were down to take a shotgun and hold armed men at bay to help him—better that she'd eliminated them, but even what she'd done had been incredibly brave and unexpected, and had probably been what had allowed him to escape that fracas without even a scratch.

"Vicente asked for us," he finally said.

That seemed to surprise her. "He did? Why?"

Quinn's mouth quirked. "He apparently lost his trust in the government of his own country long ago, and now he's lost trust in ours, as well. He knows where the cartel got many of their weapons."

"So he doesn't trust either to protect him?"

"No."

"So you are a private operation."

"Yes. Very private."

"Contracted by the government?"

"No. They called us in this time, at Vicente's demand, but we've never worked for them."

"But…how did he even know you existed?"

"We retrieved an American citizen and her daughter last year, out from under his particular drug lord's nose."

"Did the government call you in then, too?"

He grimaced. "No. And they weren't too happy when her husband did."

"You'd think they'd take all the help they could get."

"They have a tendency to be very territorial. And to think they do things best."

"Right," Hayley said, with a grimace that nearly matched his own. Then she looked about to ask another question, hesitated and asked something else. "So that's why Vicente trusted you? Because he knew you got that woman and her daughter out?"

Quinn nodded. "One of law enforcement's main focuses is their legal case, and convictions. They're spread thin that way."

"And you're different."

He nodded. "We focus on only one thing. Keeping our target alive."

She was quiet for a moment, and he could almost hear her mind working, absorbing, processing. He jumped at the chance to stop talking and start doing; he'd told her enough, and more than he ever told most people not directly involved in a case.

But then, right now she was about as involved as anybody could get. And now that Vicente's safety was out of his hands, her safety, as an innocent bystander, became paramount.

He went to work, preparing his booby traps and early-warning devices for deployment as soon as he had full cover of darkness. He's have to work fast, just in case they were also waiting for dark to attack. He'd like to think they were a bit cowed, and would take longer to regroup, but he couldn't assume that.

Hayley stood quietly, in fact handing him things as he worked. He noticed that after the first mine he didn't have to ask, she knew exactly what to give him when. If she'd been an applicant, he'd have given her a serious look, just based on how she'd handled all this.

"There are only two of us," Haley said finally. "One really. I won't be much help."

"You just keep yourself safe, let me worry about them."

"But there are more of them."

"And a lot fewer of them than they started with," he said with no small amount of satisfaction. "There's maybe five left. So odds are about even."

"Five to one is even?"

"Close enough," he said as he carefully adjusted the sensitivity of the trigger.

"Do you even know the meaning of the word 'outnumbered'?"

He glanced at her then. He hadn't realized it until that moment, but the adrenaline was building again as he dealt with the familiar weapons. These were mostly defensive, but setting them was going to be tricky, and risky.

"Nah," he said, with a grin he couldn't hold back. "Must have missed class that day."

The look she gave him made him feel an odd sort of warmth, a sensation he didn't have time to analyze just now.

Because a glance outside told him it was dark enough, and he wanted these set as soon as possible.

"Hey, dog." He said it in the exact same tone he'd been using in the conversation, no louder, with no different inflection. Yet Cutter, who had been patrolling the back of the cabin, spun instantly and trotted over to them. Yes, this was one smart, smart dog.

The animal looked up at him expectantly.

"Wanna come out and be my early-warning system again?"

The dog had been alert before, but now his head came up even more sharply, and he made that same sort of sound Quinn had heard before, a low, whuffing growl that sounded for all the world like spoken assent.

"Back," Quinn said, watching the dog. The animal spun on his right hind leg and headed for the back door.

"Testing him?"

"If I was, he passed." He started to go after the dog.

"Quinn?"

He stopped.

"Stay safe."

The use of his own words was too pointed not to be intentional.

"Both of you," she added.

Quinn couldn't stop himself; he kissed her. A brief, barely there brush of his lips, but this time it was her tempting mouth, not the relative safety of her forehead. He yanked back at the spark that seemed to leap, made himself turn away.

But she didn't protest him taking the dog this time. Telling her the truth—well, most of it anyway—had been the right thing to do, if gaining her cooperation had been the goal.

As he stepped outside, he was still trying to convince himself that that was his only goal. That telling her the truth had had nothing to do with not liking her suspecting he was one of the bad guys. Nothing to do with wanting her to keep looking at him the way she had when she'd told him to stay safe.

Nothing at all.

Chapter Twenty-Seven

It was official, Hayley thought. The boys have bonded, and she was the odd one out.

When Cutter had first dropped into her life, she'd researched the breed most knowledgeable folks told her he looked like. Intensity, a proclivity for mischief if left too long to his own devices, and the need for a job to do were high on the list. She thought she'd dealt with him fairly well; while there had been some minor incidents of doggy-style waywardness, for the most part Cutter's manners were impeccable. For a dog, anyway.

But the animal also seemed to have a madcap sense of humor, and seemed inordinately pleased whenever he made her laugh. Like the time he'd come out of her closet wearing a knit hat at a rakish angle, or—

She stopped her own thoughts as she realized she was dwelling on memories and silly things to avoid thinking about the kiss. It had been short, a mere touch of his lips on hers, but it might as well have been a marathon liplock the way her body responded. Waves of heat and sensation had swept through her, all out of proportion to the brief contact.

She thought for a moment that it was his reluctance—for he had obviously been just that—that had caused the untoward conflagration in her. Wouldn't any woman thrill to the idea of a man like Quinn driven to kiss her against his own will?

Any woman, she thought, *would thrill to the idea of Quinn kissing her, period.*

But not every woman's life was in danger, and that's what she should be thinking about, she told herself sternly. She should be thinking about what was going on in the here and now. About the fact that they could be under fire at any moment. She'd finally gotten some answers out of Quinn, but they hadn't made her feel any better. Worse, if anything. And not just because what he'd told her was grim, frightening.

Because now she was wondering if he'd finally answered her because they were likely to die here.

There's just no pleasing you, is there? she told herself sharply. It didn't help.

How on earth had she, boring, simple Hayley Cole, ended up in this mess? And no matter how she turned it over in her mind, she couldn't see herself doing anything differently than she had, couldn't see herself not going after her dog, and abandoning him to his fate when he'd dashed toward that helicopter.

But she was honest enough to realize that if she had done just that, they would likely both be safe at home right now. Quinn would probably have just ignored the dog, the helicopter would have lifted off with the intended passengers only and she would have always wondered about that strange, unmarked aircraft. From the safety of her home, with her beloved dog at her feet.

Of course, if the house had still blown up, things might have changed. She would have had to tell authorities what she'd seen then, and she'd have ended up mixed up in all this anyway, albeit from a much safer place. She would have—

A memory suddenly shot through her mind, of the first day

here, when she'd peered over the loft railing at Liam's laptop screen. Only this time it wasn't the image of the inferno that had been Vicente's home that struck her, it was the two words she'd been able to hear from her vantage point.

Explosion.

Leak.

He hadn't meant the explosion had been caused by some sort of gas leak.

Her thoughts were tumbling now, faster and faster.

He'd meant the house had been blown up because there was an information leak. And it had to be that same leak that had allowed the men outside to find them in this remote, isolated place that should have been safe.

If all the people who worked for Quinn were like the three she'd met, it was hard to believe the leak could be one of his own. In fact, she didn't believe it; those men were utterly loyal to him, and there was no reason to think he didn't inspire the same feeling in others.

It's what he inspires in you that you should be worried about.

That little voice had been nagging at her lately, and it was getting harder and harder to shut it off. And no amount of telling herself she was suffering from some variation of Stockholm syndrome had seemed to help.

And now that she knew the truth about Vicente, knew that Quinn and his crew were indeed on the side of the angels... well, she didn't know what now. And there wasn't time to figure it out.

She made herself walk around the cabin, checking every stash of weapons Quinn had left. It took her a moment to realize that he'd placed things so that no matter where you were or in what room, there was a weapon within easy reach. You'd never have to move more than five feet. And while easily accessible, some were also hidden, so that if you knew they were there you could get them without being noticed. The smaller handgun between the chair cushions, the deadly looking grenade dropped into a coffee mug, indiscernible unless you were on top of it.

She'd seen him move the sofa away from the wall then put it back, so went to look there. A large, lethal-looking knife was pinned between the back of the sofa and the wall, hilt protruding upward, and hidden by an extra pillow that looked as if it had just been put there to get it out of the way.

She spun around at the sound of Cutter's nails—she really needed to trim those, it had been on her list to do that next morning—on the floor, headed her way. Quinn was behind him, his hands empty now, his traps obviously set.

His gaze flicked from the pillow she'd just put back in place to her face. "What are you doing?"

"Believe me, if I was going to try and slit your throat, I would have done it long before now."

To her amazement, he grinned, a lopsided, heart-stealing grin like the one that had flashed when he'd cracked that joke about missing the lesson about being outnumbered. And her pulse reacted in the same way; it leaped and began to race.

The atmosphere between them changed with an almost audible snap. Became charged, heated. She lowered her eyes, but she could feel him still looking at her, could feel his gaze on her as if it were a physical thing. They were alone here now, except for Cutter, who seemed delighted to have finally gotten exactly that result.

To cover her own reaction, she hastily spoke.

"Why aren't they gone, if it's Vicente they want?"

The question had occurred to her as she was checking the various weapons. She realized it was probably wishful thinking, that they might abandon this fight to go after the man they really wanted, but it did seem a logical question to her.

"Because they don't know where he's going. Yet."

Quinn added the final word with a bite of anger; Hayley didn't envy the person who was the leak, when Quinn finally found him. And find him he would, she had no doubt of that, if for no other reason than she knew he would never give up until he did.

"But if you have a leak, they will know soon, won't they?"

He'd been loading up more explosives and trip wires into a pack, but at her words his gaze shot back to her face. "You really don't miss much, do you?"

"Happens when I figure my life depends on knowing what's going on," she said, managing to keep the sarcasm in her tone to a minimum.

To her surprise, he grinned again. Rather lopsided, but still pulse-speeding.

"You've got a knack for this, you know?"

Hayley frowned. Why was he being so nice, so normal? All of a sudden he was talking, saying nice things to her.

"Come on, Cutter dog," he said, and headed for the front door this time. He reached out and hit the light switch by the door, plunging the room into a darkness only eased by a little overflow from the kitchen. This way he wouldn't be silhouetted in the doorway, she realized, a too-tempting target for the men no doubt planning their next attack.

"Stay inside," Quinn said. And then they were gone again, man and dog. Leaving behind the woman who had just figured out the answer to her own question.

They were still here because they had an easier, faster way to find out where the man who could destroy them had been taken. They had, almost at their fingertips and certainly outnumbered, the man who had sent him there.

They were staying to get Quinn.

Chapter Twenty-Eight

She watched as Quinn slipped off the now-empty vest; he'd gotten done what he'd gone out there to do.

"So if you aren't some kind of paramilitary outfit, what are you?"

Quinn gave her a sideways glance, showing he'd heard the fourth question she'd shot at him in the same number of minutes, but again, he didn't answer.

He was cooking, quickly, in the manner of someone who doubted they'd have time later but knew they needed the fuel. He'd resorted to eggs, and tossed some other things into a big scramble in a skillet. Every now and then he'd toss a chunk of the ham he'd efficiently diced to Cutter, who caught it with ease and whuffed his thanks. When it was done, he scooped up half of it onto a plate and held it out to her.

"You should eat now."

The unspoken "because you may not get the chance later" registered, but she didn't say anything. She was too busy staring at him; he'd wrapped his share of the results in a flour tortilla, like a burrito.

"There are few foods that can't be wrapped in a tortilla," he said when he saw her look. "Less messy and more portable than a sandwich, same effect. And no dishes."

She could see his point. "Where'd you learn that?"

"My ex."

"Your ex?" she said, startled both at that bit of information, and that he'd revealed it. He seemed almost startled himself, and seemed to try to cover it with a joke.

"Hard to believe some woman actually married me, isn't it?"

The grin flashed again, and any hope she might not react so strongly to it vanished as her pulse leaped yet again. Damn the man. Never mind all the guns and grenades, that grin was his most lethal weapon. To her, anyway.

Which made her realize rather ruefully the problem wasn't him, but her.

"It's not hard to believe," she said. "Just hard to believe you ever left this job of yours long enough to marry some woman."

He seemed to hesitate, then gave a half shrug. "I didn't," he said, his voice oddly soft. "That was the problem."

So he was a workaholic? It didn't surprise her. But somehow this seemed a little different. Being fiercely dedicated to keeping someone like Vicente safe seemed different from being addicted to spreadsheets or the next microchip. But she supposed the end result was the same if you were the wife who barely saw her husband.

"So she left you? Because of your work?"

He grimaced. "Let's just say she didn't share my dedication." His tone held the finality of a man through discussing a subject he hadn't wanted to let come up in the first place. So much for the personal revelations, Hayley thought, although she longed to ask more, much more. She wanted to know who this man was, why he got under her skin so easily.

She finally took her first bite of the concoction on the plate, and was pleasantly surprised. It didn't just taste like the individual ingredients he'd mixed. Somehow the combination was savory and appetizing in a new way.

Handy guy to have around, she thought, her mouth quirking. Flies helicopters, shoots straight, good with explosives, cool under fire and he can cook, too.

"When will they attack again?"

"If they haven't already, I'm guessing they'll wait until the dead hours."

"Charming phrase."

"It's just what we call the time when most people are the most deeply asleep. Varies with the person, but two in the morning to about four or five is optimum."

"For them, you mean."

"Yes. So you should get some rest now."

"Me? Seems you should be the one resting."

"I'll be fine."

"I don't want fine. You're the one between us and them. I'd prefer well rested and ready, thank you."

He drew back sharply, his eyes widening. And then, to her shock, he laughed. It was a gravelly sort of laugh, rough, as if it didn't escape very often, and no one seemed more surprised than he did at the sound of it.

"That," he said, "was a very concise assessment."

"And true. Isn't it?"

"You're not helpless."

"I know."

"Question is, could you take that kill shot if you had to?"

"I...don't know."

"What if they hurt him?" he asked, gesturing at Cutter.

"Yes." It came out strongly, certainly. And then, without thinking, she added, "Or you."

Again surprise flashed across his face. "Me?"

"Is no one allowed to want to protect you? Is it always the other way around?"

"I don't need protecting. That's my job."

"It always comes back to that, then? Are you that wrapped up in being the big strong man, the protector, that you can't accept it from someone else?"

He took the last bite of his tortilla, ignoring her now.

"Is that also why your wife left?"

He quickly washed the skillet he'd used. Silently.

Driven by some need she didn't quite understand to break through this man's formidable defenses, Hayley pressed on. She seemed to irritate him easily enough, but now she'd gotten a laugh out of him, and she wanted more. She wanted more laughing, more smiles, that rare and precious grin. She wanted to know who he really was, why he was who he was, what had brought him here, not just to this place but to this work. She wanted to know now what drove him so hard, wanted to know if he ever stopped, what would make him stop.

She wanted his whole damned life history, inside and out, and the fact that she wanted all that so much she'd practically forgotten about the men outside and the dire situation they were in was not lost on her.

"Or could she not handle what kind of work you do? Is that the real reason she left, she couldn't deal with a man who has to arm himself to go to work?"

He put the skillet away and finally turned to look at her. "Speaking from experience?"

"It nearly split up my parents, yes," she said. "My mother had a hard time with realizing every time she sent him out the door he might not come back."

"It's a hazard of the job."

"And yours?"

"We're not talking about mine."

"I am."

"Then stop." He finished clearing the kitchen, leaving her to deal with her own plate and fork.

"Quinn—"

"Will you just leave it?"

"I can't."

He let out a compressed breath. Started to walk past her.

"I need to know."

He stopped. In front of her. Practically on top of her.

"We could die here. I need to know who you are, why you are—"

His mouth came down on hers, cutting her off. Shock immobilized her. Then, as if every nerve in her body had been jolted into awareness, heat flooded her. For an instant it seemed as if he were as stunned as she at the unexpected and sudden conflagration. But then he moved, encircling her with his arms, pressing her against him as he deepened the kiss.

Her every nerve was sizzling. She couldn't feel her knees anymore, and her arms felt heavy, weak. But it didn't matter, none of it mattered, not as long as he was there, holding her, she wouldn't fall, he wouldn't let her. All that mattered was his mouth, coaxing, probing, tasting.

It was going through her in pulses now, that heat, that surging, delicious heat, like nothing she'd ever known. Some tiny part of her brain tried to insist it was because it had been so long, but she knew it wasn't that, knew it had never been like this in her life because she'd never kissed a man like Quinn before.

No, not that, she thought as, after what seemed an eternity, he at last pulled away. Not a man *like* Quinn. Because there was no other man like Quinn, there was only Quinn.

For a moment she wished could be endless he just stood there, staring down at her. He looked as stunned as she felt. He started to speak, then stopped, as if he were rattled. He shook his head as if to clear it, and she felt a jolt of reassurance; he was feeling it, too, this huge, powerful thing that had swamped her. It wasn't one-way.

And it seemed vitally important that it not be one-way.

"Quinn," she whispered, a little startled at the low, husky sound of it.

He drew back, shook his head again, sharply this time. For a moment his fingers tightened on her shoulders. She held her breath, thinking he might pull her close for another melting kiss, then another, and—

He pushed her back. Gently but definitely.

"You—" He had to stop to clear his throat, which ameliorated the pushing away a little. He reached for a small automatic handgun from the table. "Your time would be better spent learning to handle this than asking questions I'm not going to answer."

She clung to that break in his voice, that moment when he hadn't quite been the tough, cool, unflappable Quinn. But his words were too flat, too grim to deny. The realization that she might really be in the midst of a pitched gun battle soon was beyond chilling, it sent icy tendrils curling through her, draining the wonderful heat he'd kindled.

She fought for calm, fought not to give in to the simple plea for another kiss that kept trying to rise to her lips. What was she, some weak-willed wimp of a woman, so immobilized by a man's kiss that she couldn't even think?

Yes, she admitted wryly, at this moment, she was.

She drew herself up, sucked in some air. She reached out and took the weapon from him, careful not to become a complete cliché and run her fingers over his hand. It was heavier than she'd expected, and she had to exert more effort to lift it. Then she made herself speak in a level, composed voice.

"Then teach me," she said.

For a moment he just looked at her, oddly, as if he was somehow proud of her. It warmed her even though she wasn't sure what exactly he would be proud of. Or how she'd gotten to where it mattered so much to her.

The only thing she was sure of was that kiss. And that, for now, she had to forget it. It had probably been a fluke anyway, born of adrenaline and too long alone.

And with that unsatisfying explanation, she was able to turn her mind to the matter at hand. Learning to shoot a handgun.

Learning to, if necessary, kill.

Chapter Twenty-Nine

Hayley was, Quinn thought, a lot tougher than she looked. She might seem quiet, even reserved at times, but there was a lot of fire behind that calm facade. And courage, but he'd known that all along. True, life would be easier now if she'd taken down a couple of those guys out back, but she'd held them until he took care of his own, and by then they'd thought better of their plan and scrambled back up the bluff rather than face the gutsy woman with the shotgun any longer.

And now she had set about learning the small handgun he'd given her with a fierce intensity that told him she understood what they faced. And he realized that while she might be a brand-new amateur with the Kimber, her nerve wouldn't fail, and that was more than half the battle.

She would do what she had to do. Which cut the odds against them suddenly in half.

Yes, a lot of fire....

He shook his head sharply, then again, wondering what the hell had gotten into him. The moment his mouth had touched hers he knew what had been a strategic decision had been a very, very bad one.

Quinn.

The husky whisper echoed in his mind as if the slight breeze was carrying it in an endless loop.

He'd heard his name whispered before. He'd heard it spoken, yelled, screamed. Heard it said neutrally, heard it in friendship, laughter, or anger and panic.

He'd never heard it said in a way that sent a shiver down his spine. Or made a rush of heat follow that path. Or made him wonder if his knees were going to hold out.

He steadied himself, and it was enough of an effort that it irritated him all over again.

She'd stripped, reassembled and dry-fired the weapon repeatedly, until he was sure she had it down. But nothing could prepare her for the recoil, the noise, the actual act of shooting except doing it. He figured they could spare one magazine of ammo, no more. He had to hope she was as quick at learning the actual shooting as she had been everything else. He didn't need her to be a sharpshooter, he just needed her to get close.

"Cutter?"

The dog, who had been snoozing comfortably on the couch, apparently satisfied they didn't need his supervision for this, came alert instantly. Before Quinn could say another word, Cutter was off the couch and at his side, looking up expectantly.

"Let's go do a little recon," he said, and heard the little whuffing sound he'd learned was assent. The dog couldn't possibly understand "recon," tempting though it was to think the clever guy understood perfectly, but Quinn guessed the "Let's go," was pretty clear.

"Where are you two going?"

"To pick out a firing range," Quinn said.

"But...won't that draw their attention?"

"Honey, we've got their attention, I promise you." He'd drawled it out like a joke, he'd meant it as a joke, there was no reason for her to flush as if he'd meant the endearment in the usual way. Because he hadn't. The fact that it wasn't a word he usually used even as a joke didn't change that.

"I'm actually going to go out and shoot this now?" she asked, gesturing with the pistol, carefully keeping her finger off the trigger and safely resting on the trigger guard, as he'd instructed.

"Nothing can replace actually putting rounds through it," he said. "Besides, it'll throw them off guard. Make them wonder."

She got there quickly. "You mean they'll wonder what we're shooting at?"

"Or who? If we're lucky, maybe they'll wonder if they aren't alone out here."

"Then why don't we—I—just step out and start firing?"

"I'd rather direct their curiosity somewhere else."

She looked thoughtful, then barely a second later said, "Because if they're having to watch two places, their attention will be divided."

Yes, she was quick all right.

They were maybe a couple of hundred yards from the cabin, a midnight trip that made the one that had started this whole thing seem like a stroll down a peaceful city sidewalk. The moon was full, and her nerves were screaming that they were lit up like a stage. Not only was it unfamiliar ground, but Hayley knew they were out there, watching. A fact that was pounded home when, after setting Cutter to watch their backs, Quinn told her in a harsh, low voice that she had nine minutes to get minimally familiar with firing the weapon, no more.

"A minute for them to react, five for them to figure out where they think we are, and three for them to decide what to do. If they're still where I think they are, it'll take them ten minutes to work their way over here. I want us back inside long before that."

He'd made her trade her white blouse for a dark sweatshirt, and used what looked like electrician's tape to cover her white sneakers. And he hadn't helped her over the rough ground, and she didn't know whether to be offended at his lack of assistance, or flattered that he'd been confident she could do it herself.

She'd finally decided he had enough to think about without having some needy female on his hands. But thinking about his hands immediately set her to thinking about his mouth, and there was nothing to be gained on that track except shaky hands and too-quick breathing at the memory of that unexpected, fire-inducing kiss.

She steadied herself, focusing on the target he'd laid out for her. He'd marked the side of the bluff itself with some kind of paint he'd taken from the locker, paint that put off a slight glow. The target was under an overhang that looked as if it could go at any second, which made her question the wisdom of the location, but then again, if the bluff did collapse, it would cover the target and any evidence of what they'd been doing. Better the bad guys think they were facing two expert marksmen, not one and a brand newbie.

She wasn't sure what good the target was going to do though; in the darkness of the overhang she could see the faintly glowing outline, but how on earth would she know if she was even close to hitting it?

Quinn answered the question for her as he took out what looked like a short, clunky telescope and focused it on the target. Night vision? She barely had time to wonder before he told her to fire three rounds in succession.

The moment she fired the first shot, Hayley realized three things. The kick wasn't quite as bad as she'd expected, the noise was much worse and Quinn had, not surprisingly, picked the perfect place.

Perfect because, the way the sound echoed around under the lip of this part of the bluff, she guessed from distance you'd have no idea how many shots or shooters there really were.

"You're up and to the left. Try and compensate, but don't overdo it. Three more."

She shifted her aim level and right, tried again.

"Better. Empty it."

When she was done, they headed back at a crouching run.

Cutter was out in front of them, pausing for a second or two to test the breeze before glancing back at them and starting out again, as if to make sure they'd read his all clear and were still with him. If she hadn't been looking for him, hadn't been able to spot the gleam of his dark eyes and the slightly lighter fur on his legs and lower body, the nearly black dog would have been invisible.

"You," Quinn said to Cutter when they were safely back inside, "are damned near as good as anybody I've worked with. Better than some, back in the day."

He accompanied the praise with a thorough scratch of the dog's ears. The usually cool Cutter practically wiggled with delight, managing to look smugly proud at the same time.

"How much does he understand?" Quinn asked.

Hayley smiled, despite the fact that she was in the most ominous position of her life. "I know he understands a lot. He's got an amazingly large vocabulary, for a dog. Sometimes he seems to understand context, too. Like when the wind blew my side door shut, locking my house keys inside. Now, he knows the car keys, he brings them to me, because he gets to go for a ride. But the house keys are on a different ring. I sent him through the doggy door for the car keys, because then I could unlock the car and use the garage opener. He came back with the house keys."

Quinn looked startled. He gave Cutter an assessing look, as if his opinion was shifting yet again.

"In the beginning," Hayley said, "on our vet's recommendation, I took him to obedience school. Not because he needed it, more of a bonding thing. What a waste."

"He didn't learn?"

"He didn't have to. He blew through everything in the first day, then sat there looking at me like 'Now can we go do something interesting?' The trainer asked me to bring him back so she could test him."

"Test him?"

Hayley nodded. "She started out with colors and shapes. Blue cube, red ball, yellow triangle. He got the right one every time. Then she went to a red one of each, told him what shape to get. Every time."

"Is that...unusual?"

"A bit. But then she got into trickier stuff. She'd hide stuff from him. A lot of dogs can't make the jump, for instance, that the ball you just had in your hand is now behind the chair, even if they saw you put it there. They just know it's gone. Cutter got it out of a closed box."

"Smart dog, all right."

Quinn gave the dog another sideways look as she went on. "But then it got really interesting. She showed him a picture of a rag doll. He went and got it out of a pile of toys. Same thing with a plastic bird, and a small basket, so she was pretty sure he hadn't seen any of them before."

"Hayley?"

"What?"

"Stop pacing."

She hadn't even realized she had been. Talking about Cutter, and the trainer's amazement at his intelligence, had distracted her from her worry, but her subconscious apparently hadn't forgotten that there were armed men out there waiting for their moment to strike. She wondered if that was why Quinn had let her ramble on like that.

"Sorry," she muttered, and stopped midstride. But as if her body had to do something, she felt the faintest of tremors start.

"Why don't you sit down?"

She did, mainly because she was afraid the trembling would get worse and she might simply fall down.

"Why now?" she said. "I was fine when we were outside, when we were most likely to get shot at, but now I fall apart?"

"It's natural," Quinn said with a shrug. He gave Cutter a last pat and walked over to her. He seemed even taller, towering as he stood next to the sofa. And then he sat down next to her, something he'd never done before.

Quinn looked at Cutter, who had quietly padded across the room to sit at their feet and look at them with benevolent pleasure.

"No idea where he came from?"

"Another planet is my best guess."

Quinn's gaze shot back to her. After a split second that crooked grin flashed across his face. "Now that wouldn't surprise me."

Almost involuntarily she smiled back. She had, she realized, stopped trembling. In fact, she'd felt better, calmer, since the moment he'd sat down beside her. She told herself it was simply that he was, still, distracting her from the threat outside.

Oh, he's distracting you, all right.

And what better way to spend what could be her last hours than distracted by a man like this one?

An odd sensation flooded her then, not unlike the adrenaline that had coursed through her when she'd been outside, firing that pistol at the target she could barely see. It was a sort of recklessness she'd rarely felt in her life. She wanted to know.

She needed to know.

She *had* to know.

"Quinn?"

"What?"

It took a very deep breath to steady her enough to say the words.

"Kiss me again."

For a split second he looked startled. "I'm not sure that would be a good idea."

"I don't care."

"Hayley—"

"I know you just kissed me before to stop me asking questions. Should I start asking again?"

His mouth quirked at that. But he reached out, cupped her face in his hands. She made herself fight the urge to lower her eyes, to look away. He was so damned intense, it was more difficult than she ever would have imagined simply to meet his gaze.

She was trembling again. But this time it had nothing to do with fear.

Chapter Thirty

Every instinct he had in him was screaming at him not to do it. He'd learned to trust those instincts, and more than once they had saved his life, or other lives.

Now, he wasn't fighting them.

He was ignoring them.

Because he wanted, more than he could remember ever wanting anything, to do exactly what Hayley had asked. Even knowing her simple, stunning request was born out of fear, the fear they might not survive this. He knew they had a good chance, with a certainty born of his faith in his own skills, his experience and what he knew of the disorganization of their enemy. They might run a tight ship in their criminal enterprise, but there were too many big egos for them to make an efficient fighting team.

But even knowing what was driving her didn't slow his response to her simple yet shattering request. Because he wanted to kiss her, to sample that hot, honeyed sweetness again. He wanted the taste of her, the feel of her.

Taking advantage of her fears, of the situation, would be

wrong. Unethical. She wasn't a client, so he wasn't bound by those rules, but she wasn't here willingly, either. She was trapped in a situation not of her own making, thanks to his having to make a snap decision to protect the operation.

He still wanted to kiss her. He wanted the rush of sensation that had rippled through him, seductive, addictive. He wanted to hear her say his name again, in that husky, stunned voice that sent delicious shivers racing through him like nothing in his life ever had.

Truth be told, he wanted a lot more than just a kiss. But reality was, and there wasn't going to be time for anything else.

But he would take time for this, and damn the consequences.

The tiny gasp that broke from her in the instant his lips touched hers destroyed his last reservations with a power much stronger than the faint sound warranted.

It was as hot, as fierce, as consuming as he'd remembered. And suddenly he knew why she'd asked for this. And he understood.

Then the feel of her mouth seemed to destroy his capacity for thought. He asked for more, his tongue flicking over her lips. They parted, just slightly, allowing him to probe, to taste. She was as sweet, as tempting as before, only this time his goal wasn't to quiet her questions, it was to drink all of what he'd only sipped before.

He was barely aware of what he was doing to add to the fire, stroking, caressing, knew only that the taut yet soft feel of her drew his hands onward. She moved, not to pull away but to press closer. He held her there, marveling that he'd never really noticed how incredible that womanly curve was, from hip to waist, how perfectly made for his hands.

Her fingers tightened on his shoulders, then slid down his back, leaving trails of fire behind them. And suddenly any thought that he was in control of this vanished. He'd never known anything like it, and he wasn't sure it could be controlled. He wasn't sure he wanted to control it.

And that alone should have scared the hell out of him, he

who had spent his adult life and half his childhood trying to do just that, control every circumstance. But it didn't scare him, he was too revved up, too pumped to allow fear to take hold. More than he'd ever been in any battle, anywhere.

And then her tongue began its own hesitant exploration and his muscles clenched in response, so fiercely he was vaguely surprised his bones didn't snap. His body was on full alert, ready to discard reality and take what it wanted. It was a feeling he'd never experienced before, a consuming, fiery need he wouldn't have believed existed if he weren't being swallowed up by it himself.

He felt an odd sensation at his waist, realized her hands had slid downward and were tugging at his shirt. Just that knowledge threatened to destroy the last little bit of his control. As if her actions invited his, he slid his hands up beneath the soft sweatshirt, savoring the silken skin, feeling the slight ridges of her ribs. He reached the curve of her breasts, felt the soft flesh round into his palms. He groaned, unable to stop the escape of the harsh, almost helpless sound.

Cutter barked. Quietly. It sounded odd, almost reluctant, as if he didn't want to interrupt them with that reality.

Reality.

A tiny part of his trained mind that was still functioning sent up a warning, a warning he'd ignored until now.

With a tremendous effort he broke the kiss. Hayley's small sound of protest sent shivers through him, and nearly sent him straight back to her sweet, soft mouth.

But Cutter barked again, still sounding reluctant, yet more definite this time.

Quinn looked at the dog. If it was possible for a dog to look apologetic, this one was doing it. The moment he saw Quinn looking at him, the animal trotted across to the front corner of the cabin, then looked back.

As clearly as if he'd spoken, Quinn understood the dog's message.

They're coming.

Reality slammed back into him like an iceberg, and that lovely, burgeoning heat vanished.

"It's them, isn't it?" she asked, her eyes starting to refocus, but still touched with the remnants of that exploding heat.

He nodded. He sat up, ordering a body resistant to the abrupt cessation of the most pleasure it had ever known, to stand down. There was a battle coming, and he couldn't let this, whatever the hell it was, cloud his thinking.

Nor could he resist reaching out and lifting her chin with a gentle finger.

"Hayley."

It was a voice he'd never heard from himself, a voice full of longing, need and promises he'd never made before.

She met his gaze, steadily, and he could almost see her gathering herself to deal with what was coming. Admiration spiked through him. Yes, she would do, he thought.

"It wasn't a fluke, Hayley."

Surprise flashed in her eyes, confirming his guess that this was what had been behind her request. Not that it changed anything. He spared a split second for regret, knowing full well that when this was over she'd likely want to walk away and never think of this, and that he would have to let her.

But first, he had to keep her alive to do it.

She'd been wobbly at first, as if Quinn's strength-sapping kiss had somehow liquefied her bones. But Cutter, now that he'd interrupted them, was indicating they had little time before the enemy was upon them, pacing anxiously by the door, growling, casting impatient glances at Quinn.

But she was steadier now. Something about the act of picking up a handgun you actually expected to have to use did that, she guessed.

Quinn had given her a holster that clipped onto the waistband of her jeans, and she slipped the small semiautomatic into it. She slipped on the vest he'd given her as well, then took up the shotgun.

When she was done, he was already at the door. He'd suited

up quickly, wearing his own vest of a different kind, loaded with weaponry and ammo. Cutter was dancing at his feet in his eagerness to get at it. Two of a kind, she thought, her throat tight.

"This could get nasty," he said. "Maybe you should get in the bedroom now and—"

"Don't even think about it."

She said it with more bravado than she was really feeling, and was surprised it sounded so steady and determined. But the upward quirk at the corner of Quinn's mouth was reward enough for much more than a declaration of a strength she wasn't sure she really possessed.

"Hang on to him." He gestured at Cutter. "I need to get to the windmill."

"You've witnessed how well that works when he's determined," she pointed out. "Why the windmill?"

"High ground. And as clever as he is, I doubt he can climb that narrow ladder."

"I'll try."

"Lock up after me."

She nodded.

He reached for the door. For an instant he paused, looking back at her. Their gazes locked, and something deep and primal and undeniable leaped between them, as if the connection were a living, breathing thing.

He moved as if he were going to kiss her again, and Hayley's pulse leaped. At the last second he stopped himself.

"Later," he muttered. It seemed he said it as much to that vivid connection as to her.

And then he was gone into the night.

Chapter Thirty-One

Cutter lasted until the first explosion.

It was distant, probably one of the mines Quinn had set, but the dog didn't care. He clawed at the door his idol had left through, clawed at the knob, trying to turn it with his paws. He whined, so loudly and insistently it tore at her. She went to try to calm him, but he spun away from her. From a yard away he stared at her, then the door, intensity radiating from him.

I have to go, I need to help him.

Hayley shook her head sharply. If the situation weren't so dire, she'd laugh at herself for putting human thoughts into a dog's head, even if that look in his eyes was more commanding than she'd ever seen in some humans, let alone an animal. No wonder sheep did what he wanted; it was all she could do not to herself, not to just open the door and let him out there.

Another explosion—was it closer, or was that her imagination?—sounded. Still Cutter stood there, silently demanding she let him out into the melee.

Quinn would understand, she thought. Whatever code he

lived by, it didn't include staying behind while others fought. Apparently Cutter lived by the same code. And at this moment it didn't even seem ridiculous to think that a dog had a code.

A third explosion. Definitely closer. And this time it was followed by the sound of gunfire. Not the rapid automatic-spray technique of their attackers, just steady, single shots fired with calm purpose. Rafer Crawford might be the team sniper, but Quinn was no slouch.

She heard several shots before the automatic return fire started. Bursts of it, fired by men whose strength came from firepower instead of skill. The steady, calm response of Quinn's shots continued; obviously he wasn't rattled by the attack.

Cutter, on the other hand, was about to claw his way through the door. She crouched beside the frantic dog.

"I know you want out there, but it's too dangerous, you need to stay here, where it's safe."

The dog gave her a swipe of his tongue over her cheek, as if in appreciation for the sentiment, but went right back to clawing at the door.

The next explosion was much, much closer. It had to be, it was so much louder. Cutter barked, a booming, angry sound. He looked at her, again with that demanding expression in those expressive eyes.

Out of nowhere a thought hit her. That explosion. Had it been louder because it was closer?

Or louder because it wasn't a mine, muffled by the earth around it?

She ran to the window. The now-familiar tableau was painted an eerie silver by the moonlight. She could just see the edge of the windmill, the high ground Quinn had headed for. And several feet off the ground, smoke curled out from one of the vertical legs. Even as she looked, something flew through the air and hit the leg. Another explosion, bright yellow flames a shocking burst of color in the silver light. More smoke and some debris burst from the base of the tower.

Explosives. The man draped like a suicide bomber.

They were trying to take it down. Apparently unable to get any closer because of Quinn's deadly accurate aim, they were trying to take it down with explosives, lobbed from a safe distance. She couldn't see them, both because they were far enough away and they were out of the field of vision of the small window.

If they managed to collapse that leg, the whole thing would go. With Quinn in it.

The sound of Cutter running spun her around. The dog was headed toward the back door. She called to him, but he kept going. Much as he had that night this had all began.

She watched in shock as the dog reached the door, reared up on his hind legs and batted at the lever-style handle with his front paws. She started toward him, but before she got there he had gotten enough pressure on the handle to release the lock. The crazy dog had opened the door.

"Cutter, no!"

His dark head turned, and he gave her a look she could only describe as apologetic. And then he was gone, racing into the fray with all the determination of the man he was following.

For an instant she just stood there, staring at the empty place where the dog had been. The sounds of more gunfire and another explosion echoed from the bluff just outside the now-open back door. If that door hadn't had that lever-style handle, Cutter would still be safely inside. She should have known the too-clever dog would figure out that he could open it if he just got his paws in the right place. And she had inadvertently aided his escape by not immediately throwing the dead bolt on that door.

She didn't do it now. Anybody who came through that door who wasn't Quinn or Cutter she was going to shoot, she thought with determination. She darted to the small, lens-style window. Cutter was racing down the open space at the foot of the bluff in an odd, zigzagging pattern it took her a moment to figure out. When she did, her breath caught; he was dodging the mines Quinn had buried. As if he not only knew the threat they posed, but remembered where each and every one was.

To her surprise he headed, not toward the windmill and Quinn, but to the south. He skidded to a halt just past the outcropping of rock that had sheltered Quinn and him before. He crouched there, looking ready to pounce, his gaze and that powerful nose pointed upward.

Her fingers tightened around the shotgun still in her hand. Quinn could handle himself, as she'd seen. He was a dangerous man, a formidable opponent. And he was armed and ready, trained to fight against just such an enemy as this. She knew that as surely as she knew his eyes were blue, even if she didn't know where he'd gotten that training.

Cutter, on the other hand, was a dog. An impossibly smart, clever and resourceful dog, but still, just a dog. Something she had to force herself to remember at times like this, when he seemed to exhibit an intelligence far beyond ordinary canine capabilities.

The tumble of a rock down the bluff, just a few feet away, brought her out of the reverie she could ill afford. Her gaze shot upward, just in time to see a rope coming over the lip of the bluff to the south. And she realized with a shiver that Cutter hadn't headed for Quinn because he knew they were closer than that.

They weren't just trying to take down Quinn's tower.

They were coming after her.

Chapter Thirty-Two

They would kill Cutter. Because he would try to stop them. She had no doubts about that. Just as she no longer had any doubts about the nature of this enemy. The story Quinn had told her had made it clear they were merciless, and would do anything to get what they wanted.

And what they wanted was in Quinn's head. Anything or anyone else was just in the way.

But she wasn't in the way. She was here, and if she'd been thinking clearly enough, Cutter still would be, too. So why were they coming after her? Why bother, when she was so obviously harmless?

They'd been hurt, badly, by Quinn and his men in their first attack. They had to know it would take everything they had left to get to him. For all the good it would do, he would never tell them a thing. She knew that down to her bones, although it made her shudder inwardly to think of what they might do to him to try to get him to talk. What they might use on him to—

It hit her then. They wanted her, to use on him. They might

not know what she was to him—couldn't know, since she herself didn't—but they did have the measure of the man. And somehow they knew he was the kind of man who would never allow an innocent to be hurt if he could stop it.

They wanted her for leverage.

For an instant she felt a flash of relief at the realization that for that, they'd need her alive. In the next instant, self-disgust filled her. Had she always been such a coward? Quinn had risked his life to keep Vicente safe, and now was risking it for her; she had belatedly realized he wasn't in that tower just for the high ground, but to lead them away from her.

Cutter barked, and she heard a shot. Close. Too close.

She grabbed up an extra box of shotgun shells and shoved them into the one empty vest pocket that remained. She yanked the door handle until it unlatched. She kicked the door open, simultaneously putting both hands back on the shotgun, ready to fire.

Cutter had dug in, literally, behind and below the outcropping. Amazingly, he was in a place where the angle made it impossible for anybody from above to get a clear shot at him. Did he somehow sense that?

This was not the time to dwell on the wonders of this particular canine mind. She could see the tracks Cutter had left in the dry dirt, thrown into stark relief by the moonlight. It didn't really matter whether he knew where the mines were, or maybe smelled them, he'd gotten through and therefore his was the path she should follow.

Assuming the mines just weren't set so that his slighter weight wouldn't trigger them....

She shook off the thought. It didn't matter. She'd had enough of this, enough of being a helpless pawn in all this.

"God made man, Sam Colt made them equal." She tightened her grip on the shotgun as she whispered Quinn's words. "Or in this case, Mr. Mossberg."

She made her way through Quinn's minefield safely, thanks to Cutter trailblazing the way. The dog's ears swiveled, and she knew he heard her coming. But he never looked away from the vertical outcropping, as if he expected someone to pop out any second.

And if he did, she thought, he probably had very good reason. This was Cutter, after all.

She thought quickly. The back of the cabin and thus her position was also out of the range of vision of anyone on the other side of the rocks. Here in the shadows no way they could see her, even with moonlight pouring down, without sticking their head out. Out into her line of fire.

And if they were looking somewhere else....

"A little noise would be good, dog," she whispered, wishing the dog would bark again from his protected spot, draw their attention.

She knew he couldn't have heard her, but in that moment Cutter let out a trumpeting volley of barking like she'd never heard from the dog before. If she hadn't been so focused, she would have been staring at him in surprise.

A head and shoulders popped up like a tin target in a county fair shooting gallery. Hayley had always been good at those. And her eyes were completely adjusted to the silver light now. The man aimed a handgun in Cutter's direction. She snapped the shotgun to her shoulder and fired in one smooth, easy motion. A satisfying yelp echoed off the back of the cabin. The next thing she saw was a pair of feet in ridiculously shined boots and a set of back pockets over a skinny backside as her target tried to scramble back. She peppered the backside just because, and heard a string of curses that she was guessing called into question her parentage and her occupation.

Much easier than skeet, really, she thought, barely suppressing a grin. "Shoot at my dog, will you," she muttered.

Cutter was quiet now, and back to looking up. The rope over the lip of the bluff moved slightly, and Hayley lifted the shotgun once more. She'd lose efficiency at that distance, and she'd have to compensate for shooting at such a sharp angle, but she could still make anyone who looked over in response to the injured man's yells very sorry.

Someone did, a round-faced man who looked as if this was

the last place he wanted to be. She reinforced the feeling with two quick shots that took the edge of the bluff almost out from under him, and she hoped from his yell, had put his right arm out of action.

Her breath caught in her throat when Cutter suddenly burst from his cover and headed back toward her. He paused for barely a second, just long enough for her to run a hand over his head, and for him to give her a wet-nosed nudge. And then he was moving again, heading around the corner of the cabin.

Heading for Quinn.

She glanced back, but there was no more sound of movement except for the first man crawling painfully away, scuffing his shiny shoes in his effort to move with shotgun pellets in his backside. And then a volley of gunfire, so many shots in succession she couldn't count them, came from the direction Cutter had gone.

She swiftly replaced the fired shells. Then she followed her dog.

The moment she rounded the corner of the house, she saw Quinn had a problem; the wooden leg of the windmill was burning, and the flames were climbing the rickety-looking structure at an alarming rate. She guessed the thing was reinforced, as was everything around here, but that didn't mean the smoke alone couldn't kill him.

Cutter apparently sensed the danger as well, because once again he ran a crazy, zigzag pattern across the open space to get to Quinn.

A shot rang out from somewhere near the barn. Cutter yelped and went down.

Hayley screamed.

Cutter struggled to get up, drawing another shot. This time she saw where it came from. It was the human-size door in the big sliding barn door nearest her. In the crouching kind of run she'd seen Quinn use, she made it to the old, rusted-out tractor. She braced herself against the rotted seat. Gauged the angle from there to where Cutter lay, figured he had to be on the side to her right. She fired three rounds in rapid succession, spacing them from knee height to head height on that side. The spread of shot was a good seven feet by three.

For an instant she held her breath. She heard what sounded like a piece of metal hit the ground, followed by a faint thud. Just the sound she'd have expected from a dropped weapon and a wounded man falling. Maybe dead, she wasn't sure she cared, not looking over at where Cutter lay, helpless, maybe dying....

She took a step toward her dog. A loud pinging sound echoed from the tractor. A bullet; somebody had obviously spotted her. Not surprising after all the noise she'd made.

But she had to get to Cutter. He wasn't dead, he just needed help, he couldn't be dead, not Cutter. He was too alive, too vital, too clever.

The moment she moved again another shot hit the tractor, this time shearing off a piece of metal that sliced at her cheek. She was effectively pinned down.

"Cutter!" she screamed, watching, telling herself she really had seen the dog move in response.

And then, out of the swirling smoke of the burning tower, came Quinn. He dropped the last ten feet as if it were nothing. He crouched, spun to his left. Fired several rounds at the far side of the barn, where the shots at her had come from. In the same smooth motion he grabbed something from his vest pocket and straightened, then lobbed it with amazing accuracy toward the same spot.

The explosion made her jump, even though she'd known it was coming. That corner of the barn blew inward, fire and smoke billowing.

And Quinn ran straight for Cutter. She heard more shots, from farther out, someone who must have been clear of the barn. Quinn jerked once, but kept going. In seconds he had scooped up the dog from the dirt.

He was helpless now, Hayley realized, with his arms full of dog. And, she saw with a sick feeling, he was hurt himself; a dark stream was flowing rapidly from his left shoulder. She had to cover their retreat. She stepped out from behind the tractor, firing toward the corner of the barn to where those last rounds had come from. Quinn passed her, Cutter cradled in his arms.

She kept firing, with each shot taking a step backward, toward the cabin. She emptied the shotgun, took the chance to swiftly reload three more shells, then fired again, although now it was for show and noise more than effectiveness at this distance.

"Get inside!"

She heard Quinn's yell, but her blood was up and she wasn't quite through with the pigs who had hurt her dog. She fired her last two shells. Then she heard the rapid, steady fire of a big rifle, coming from behind her, and knew Quinn was back in the fight. Only then did she do as he'd ordered.

"About time," Quinn said.

She was about to snap at him when she realized the words hadn't been directed at her. Then she heard a new, glorious sound. A helicopter. If not the same one, then a twin, shiny, black, unmarked and lethal looking.

And this one was wearing teeth, large-caliber rounds chewing up all in its path.

And in the distance, a faint line of light marked the coming of sunrise.

It was over.

Chapter Thirty-Three

"Take it easy with him! He's been as much a part of this fight as any of us."

Hayley heard Quinn's order, snapped across the room from where Rafer, who had led the new team in, was applying a tidy field dressing on his upper left arm. She wanted to go to him, to embarrass him in front of everyone with a huge hug for those words, but she couldn't and wouldn't move until she knew Cutter was going to be all right. She petted him steadily in reassurance.

"Yes, sir," Teague said as he ran his hands over the dog lying on the couch where Quinn had put him when they'd staggered inside just as the cavalry had arrived. "I've stood enough guard shifts with him to know he's one of us."

Surprisingly, Quinn's wound filled her with an entirely different emotion; he'd gotten it saving her dog, he'd risked his life—and taken a bullet—doing it. But he'd kept coming, never wavering, his goal the dog, and getting him out of the line of fire. Any lingering doubts she had about the man had vanished with that act.

She waited, her thoughts so occupied by the two injured males in the room that she was only barely aware of the change in atmosphere, the new quiet and calm that had settled in. It truly was over. And so quickly she was still a little stunned; the ubiquitous and all-knowing Charlie had apparently had backup on standby from the moment they'd gone dark.

"I think he'll be okay," Teague said as he cleaned the ugly-looking furrow, while Cutter bore it stoically, as if he understood that despite the pain Teague was helping him. "It looks like it's as much a graze as anything to me. There'll be a vet standing by when we land."

"Thanks, Teague," she said.

"Thank Quinn, he ordered it."

She sucked in a breath as Rafer came up behind her shoulder. "He stays cool, uninvolved because he has to," he said to her softly, and she knew he wasn't talking about Teague. "If he gave his heart to every case, it would kill him. It's not that he doesn't care, he cares too much."

She looked sideways at the lean, rangy sniper. "I see that now."

"Problem is, he's forgotten how to let himself off the leash. Maybe you could teach him that."

Before she could think of a thing to say to that, the man had turned and gone.

Once Teague was done, Cutter began to gingerly get to his feet. Hayley tried to coax him to lie back down, but Quinn was there now, on his own feet, and stopped her.

"Best to let him, if he can."

Slowly she stood up, and watched as Quinn, now in a one-sleeved shirt and a tightly bandaged arm that matched Cutter's side, crouched down to the dog's level, laid a hand on his head and looked him straight in the eyes.

"You're a good man, Cutter Cole."

The whimsy of him giving the dog her last name made her smile. It seemed to please Cutter inordinately; his thick plume of a tail began to wag.

"My two wounded warriors," she said softly, barely aware of saying it aloud.

Quinn straightened, looked at her. She braced, waiting for him to chew her out for leaving the cabin. And then it hit her. It really was over. She was no longer an unintended hostage.

"Yes," she said abruptly. "I came outside."

"You did," Quinn said, without heat.

"You're not my father, to order me. Or my husband, to suggest. Or even my boyfriend, to request."

"I could work on that," he said, his voice still startlingly mild. "Except for the father part, of course."

She gaped at him. He looked suddenly unsettled, as if he hadn't meant to say that.

"You did what you thought you had to," he said, briskly now. "And as it turned out, it was a good thing you did. I didn't think they had enough men left to come at us effectively from two flanks."

Mollified, even pleased, she said, "There were only the two in back."

"And you took out one and sent the other scrambling."

"Cutter showed me where they were."

Quinn glanced down and smiled. The dog was sitting now, dead center between them, looking from one to the other as each spoke. "Good man," he said again, and the dog gave him his best doggy grin. Quinn laughed. And again it transformed his face. It took her a moment to think of something safe to say.

"Vicente is safe?" she asked.

"He is. As is his family. We pulled them out three hours ago."

"Good. He's a brave man."

"Yes."

"As are you."

"I have a good team."

"Not one of whom was here when you risked your life to save Cutter."

"He'd earned it. I meant what I said, he was as much a part of this fight as we were."

"But he's still just a dog."

"I'm no more sure of that than you are."

She blinked; she hadn't expected that.

"We're ready, sir," Teague said.

This time when she boarded the sleek, black helicopter, Hayley did it willingly. And this time, she was the one on the floor with Cutter, while Quinn sat and watched them both.

They lifted off into the dawn sky.

"Who are you? Will you tell me now?"

"Hayley—"

"I think we've earned that, Cutter and I."

He studied her for a long, silent moment. They were in an office on the top floor of an unmarked, three-story building in a clearing hidden by a thick forest of evergreens. It felt more like home to her than the barren, rolling land they'd left, but the presence of an apparent office building out in this rural area, with a helipad and a large warehouse the only other structures, seemed odd.

Quinn turned to Rafer and Teague, who seemed to be carefully not looking at them. "Rafe, let Charlie know what needs to be replaced and fixed at the cabin. Teague, go lock down the chopper."

The two men exchanged a look Hayley thought a little pointed, but they left without comment. Liam, Teague had told her, was closeted with Vicente, still taking down the details of his long, bloody story.

Quinn turned back to her. He gestured at the couch on the far wall, a resigned expression on his face.

She wondered why it was so hard, now that it was over, to just explain. But she sat, ready to settle in for a long story, if that's what it was. Cutter was safely in the care of a kind-eyed vet who had gone all soft at the dog's story; Hayley had trusted him instantly. And had smiled inwardly at the way Quinn had automatically leaned down and lifted the dog gently onto the examining table, and more at how he'd stroked the dog's head and assured him that he'd be okay, and that they'd be back to pick him up in a few hours.

For an instant she'd even thought the dog had pulled back a little, as if he wanted to look at the two of them together. Then he made a whuffing sound that she'd swear held a note of satisfaction, and lay down to await the vet's ministrations.

Normally, Hayley would have stayed at the vet's, but she had too many questions that demanded answers, and she wasn't about to let Quinn out of her sight until she had them. Now, he sat down beside her.

"Who are you?" she asked again when he didn't speak.

"We're a private foundation. We work on referral only."

She'd meant who was he, personally, but she figured they'd get there, and she wanted to know this, too. She wanted to know everything. And she was past worrying about what that meant.

"Protecting witnesses?"

"Not usually. This was a special case, because Vicente insisted on us. Mostly it's other things."

"Like the kidnap victim you saved."

"That was actually unusual, too, but yes."

"What else?"

He let out a compressed breath. "We take on jobs nobody else will. For people who have nowhere else to turn, or who have been let down by the people supposedly there to help."

"Like the police?"

"Sometimes…although it's usually not the cops, but the brass who have things mucked up. Or some politician who's decided what's politically expedient. And we're strictly domestic, unless a case has elements elsewhere, like the kidnapping that brought us to Vicente's attention."

"What about the military?"

"That's a pool we don't swim in. We don't do military-contract work, if that's what you're asking."

"But you're all ex-military?"

"No. Liam, for example, isn't. It's not a requirement."

"What is?"

"That you be the best at what you do."

"This team of yours here—"

"Is one of three security teams we can field. We also have a tech team, a couple of investigative teams, a transportation team and a couple of others."

Her idea of the size of this operation suddenly shifted. "That's a lot."

"We started out small, but the demand grew."

"These...private cases?"

"We tend to call them lost causes," he said.

She liked that idea. "Who runs this foundation? Who started it?"

"My...family. What's left of it."

"Quinn?"

"What?"

"Just start at the beginning. Please."

"I'm not sure where that is." He ran a hand through tousled hair. "We formed the foundation four years ago. But I guess we really started in 1988."

"What happened in 1988?"

He looked at her then, and she had the oddest feeling he was watching for her reaction to what he was about to say.

"Lockerbie."

Her breath caught. "The bombing?" She'd only been a small child when it had happened, but even so she remembered her parents' horror, the nightmare photographs she'd seen since.

He nodded. "My parents were on that plane."

I was ten.... She just stared at him as his words echoed in her head. Memories swirled, including the later, hideous findings that it was likely some of the passengers had survived the explosion and died on impact. What could she possibly say in response to such horror?

"I knew I had to become a soldier, to fight back."

"And you did. Marines, like Teague and Rafer?"

He smiled. "No, but I like them anyway. Second Ranger Battalion."

That didn't surprise her; she'd already seen he was a well-trained warrior. "But you left?"

"I quit," he said, his voice so grim it sent a chill through her, "the day they let that son of a bitch go."

"The bomber," she breathed, remembering all the controversy a few years ago about backroom deals, talk of a compassionate release for a dying man with mere months to live, who was alive and apparently quite well years later. "You must have been outraged."

"Beyond. I knew I'd never again really trust the men in charge after that. The injustice destroyed my faith."

Hayley drew back slightly. "That's it, isn't it? That's what you're doing."

"What?" he asked, and again she had that feeling he was testing her somehow, waiting for her answer.

"Injustice. That's why the 'lost causes.' You're doing what should be done but isn't."

He smiled then, so warmly she wondered that she could ever have thought him cold. She felt as if she'd done something wonderful, and she didn't even know what.

"We work for people in the right, who haven't been able to get help anywhere else. Or who can't afford to fight any longer."

The simple words tugged at something deep inside her, reminded her of what it felt like to have a sense of purpose, something she'd lost in her life when her mother died. Something she had missed, without realizing that's what she was missing.

"You mean…you do it for nothing?" she asked.

"The Foxworth Foundation is self-supporting, yes."

"How?" She gestured in the general direction of the building that now housed the sleek black helicopter that had started it all. "This can't be cheap."

"We started out with quite a bit of money from our folks, and we have a genius at investment at the financial helm, somebody who keeps it growing and makes the occasional figurative killing."

"Sounds like a good person to have around."

"She is."

"She?"

"My sister."

She blinked. "Your sister?"

"She was fourteen when they died. We went to live with our only living relative. Mom's brother. We had money our parents had left us, so we weren't a burden, but Uncle Paul wasn't a kid kind of guy. He tried, but it was mostly my sister who raised me."

"Obviously she did a fine job."

He blinked. "I... You..."

For the first time he looked utterly flummoxed, and Hayley took no small pleasure in that.

A sharp knock on the door interrupted her enjoyment.

"All locked down here, sir. Charlie wants reports ASAP, of course, and asked if it was you who needed the vet."

Teague said it with a grin, Quinn reacted with a grimace. "Tell Charlie I appreciate the concern. The reports'll get there when they get there. You guys are clear."

Teague looked from Quinn to Hayley and back. He looked as if he were trying to hide another grin. "What about Hayley?"

"I'll get her home."

"And are you going to—"

"Just leave me a vehicle," Quinn said, an edge creeping into his voice. "Go home. Get some rest. You've all earned it."

When they'd gone, Hayley made no move to get up. Quinn looked at her warily, as if aware he'd dodged the real intent of her first question.

"Where's home for you?" she asked.

"At the moment, St. Louis."

"That's a ways."

"It's central. When we started, we needed that. But now we've got setups like this here—" he gestured around them "—and in three other regions, too. So we can respond more quickly. We'll be putting team leaders in all of them."

She noticed he'd responded with an answer about his work, not his life away from work. If there was such a thing.

"Is that where your sister lives, too, St. Louis?"

"Yes. She's happy there."

"But you're not?"

He shrugged. "I'm more of a cool-weather guy. Humidity kills."

She smiled. "You'd like it here then. Most of the time."

"I do like it here. I was here when the call came in for Vicente."

It felt odd to her, that he had been here in her neck of the woods and she hadn't known. He commanded so much space, it almost seemed to her she would have somehow sensed his presence.

Her mind was racing, absorbing and underneath it all ran a relieved delight, not just that he wasn't the bad guy she'd feared that night, but that he was one of the very good guys, doing work she could respect and admire. Perhaps on some level she'd known it all along. Why else would she have had the nerve to get in his face all the time?

Which was a good thing, since the vivid, unquenchable memory of his kiss had surged into her mind with undeniable force.

"Quinn," she said, then stopped, uncertain what to say.

She saw by the change in his expression that he'd read her easily.

"Hayley, I'm sorry you got sucked into this. I know now we can trust you to not say anything until the hearings are over and Vicente is safe in his new life."

"Of course," she said, "but that's not—"

"Someone will let you know when that is, in case you miss the news."

She didn't bother to ask how they'd find her number, knowing they probably already had it. "All right, but—"

"You know it was he who insisted you have the run of the cabin, while he stayed hidden. He felt responsible for you getting sucked up into this."

"I know he's a good man. But it's you I—"

"Let's pick up Cutter and get you both back home."

He moved as if he were going to stand up and leave right now.

"Just like that? It's over?" She sucked in a breath and made herself say the one thing she knew he was trying not to hear. "What happened between us—"

"Is impossible, Hayley." The only thing that kept her from being furious was the genuine regret in his voice. "You were caught up in a nightmare situation, you handled it incredibly well, now it's time to go home."

She ignored the compliment. "Why is it impossible?"

"Because it wasn't real, not really. You were scared, in danger, that does strange things to your psyche."

"So I just imagined that meltdown that happens when we kiss?"

His eyes closed. She saw his lips part as he drew in a deep breath. She relished every sign that he wasn't as cool and calm as he tried to appear. Not about this.

"No," he said softly, in the tone of a man who wished he could say otherwise. He could have lied, Hayley thought, but he didn't. Her pulse kicked up another notch.

He opened his eyes and met her gaze. "My life is crazy. I'm always going from place to place. Most times it's routine, but sometimes it's like this was, dangerous. It's not a life anybody would want to share." He shook his head slowly, lowered his gaze, rubbed at his forehead as if weariness was finally catching up with him. "I've tried. It just doesn't work."

"I'm sure it would be difficult. It would take the right person. Somebody who understood why it has to be the way it is."

"I won't ask any woman to put up with it. Not again. And I can't stop doing it."

"No!" It broke from her so loudly it startled even her. "No," she repeated, more normally. "You're doing a great thing, you can't stop."

"Easy to say when you haven't had to live with it. It's time for you to get back to your life."

"I had no life," she said, not realizing until the words came out how true they were. "I was treading water, floundering, since my mom died. Going through the motions. No job to go back to, no work that interested me."

"Applying for a job with us?"

"Would you give me one?"

He grimaced. "I think that might complicate things even more."

"You mean…because of this?"

She leaned in, before he had a chance to pull back, and kissed him. For an instant he stiffened, but so quickly it soothed her nerves and calmed her uncertainty, he responded, making a low sound that thrilled her as his hands came up to her shoulders and pulled her close. The fire that had only been banked flared up fiercer than ever, and this time Hayley let it burn, in fact stoked it as best she knew how, not caring if she looked foolish or inexperienced, risking it all on the certainty that what she was feeling had to be mutual.

Quinn slid back on the sofa, pulling her on top of him. She went, eagerly, kissing him harder, deeper, loving every groan she ripped from him, every tightening of his fingers on her, every arching move of his aroused body against her that proved she was right.

When at last she pulled back he was gasping.

"That," she said unsteadily, "is something else I didn't have in my life. Have never had. Because it's something rare, special."

"I know," he said, looking a little shell-shocked. "I wish—"

"Don't wish. You of all people should know that's for kids."

Something odd flashed in his eyes then. "Yes, I do know."

"Then you should also know this—us—is too special to walk away from."

"I never said I wanted to walk away." He tightened his arms around her. "God, who the hell would want to walk away from *this?*"

"Then don't."

"But—"

"You need to just listen. I want purpose in my life. I lost that for a while, but I've found it again now. I need that kind of goal, to do the right thing. The kind of thing that used to be the rule, not the exception."

His eyes had widened slightly, and he opened his mouth as if to speak. She put a finger on his lips, hushing him.

"You said I was strong, that I handled this better than you ever would have expected. I can handle what you sometimes have to do. I would love to help you in your work. But I need you more. If I can't have both, and I have to choose, I choose you."

"Ah, God, Hayley, you're killing me."

"Don't walk away from this. From us. You're not asking me to put up with it. I'm volunteering."

He reached up and smoothed back a strand of her hair. His mouth quirked. "I meant that literally. If you don't move I may never be able to…show you how much what you said means to me."

She realized suddenly her leg was pressing rather definitely against a very rigid and highly sensitive part of him. She nearly jumped, but he seemed to sense it and grabbed her in time to stop the sudden move that might have made things worse.

"Easy. I have plans for that later."

She was so embarrassed it took her a moment to process the change in him. She lifted her head to look at him, saw in those blue eyes that seemed so readable now the truth of what had just happened. Quinn had given up fighting her.

"Just like that, you surrender?" She wasn't quite sure she believed it, and it echoed in her voice.

"Maybe my heart wasn't really in the fight," he said. "Maybe I wanted to surrender all along."

Hayley's heart began to pound, so hard she marveled he couldn't hear it.

"You're the most amazing woman I've ever met, Hayley

Cole. And you're right. What happens between us is too rare to turn my back on. And maybe...maybe you *can* deal with it."

"I dealt with it when I had no idea what the heck was going on. Imagine what I could do if I knew the plan."

That won a smile from him, and Hayley felt it was no small victory.

And then he was kissing her, and all thoughts of plans vanished, leaving only victory and surrender, and the sweetness of sharing both equally.

They were late picking up Cutter, but the dog didn't seem to mind at all.

Quinn woke with the pleasant knowledge that his arm was merely tender, not aching, and the far beyond merely pleasant knowledge that Hayley was curled up against him. The room was pleasantly cool, and the predawn air held the promise of the impending winter. He'd been happy to find she liked to sleep as he did, warm and snug in a cold room.

Oh, and naked. There was that, too. She'd told him she'd had to resort to pajamas when she'd been running to check on her mother at all hours, but now she seemed to have forgotten where she'd put them, and he wasn't about to complain.

He'd never known such unending sweetness. Whether he woke her in the night, hot and needy, or even better, she woke him in the same condition, or they came together in the daylight, in the morning in her big shower, the afternoon on the big couch or the evening in her bed, it was hotter and more imperative than anything he'd ever known, or even known was possible.

He even liked the cuddling afterward. Of course, that'd she'd told him to think of it as foreplay for the next time helped, he thought now with a grin into the faint light of dawn.

"Going to do something with that, or waste it?"

Her sleepy voice was accompanied by a delicious wiggle of her hips against flesh that had been well aware of her closeness long before he'd actually awakened.

"Got any suggestions?" he whispered against her hair.

"I'll think of something."

He laughed, and pulled her closer. And then, so easily, so perfectly, he was sliding into her. A groan of pleasure rippled up from deep in his chest, and he marveled again how it always seemed new, fierce, intense. Deeper, long slow strokes, until she went wild beneath him, driving him wild in turn, until the moment when she cried out his name and sent him spiraling out of control with the clenching of her body.

Much later, when he normally would have been back to sleep, he instead was thinking of the day to come. It had been a quiet, healing, lovely week, enough to tell him that he should seriously consider this as his permanent location. He'd even managed to, temporarily, put the mole out of his mind. But this afternoon he was taking her to St. Louis, to see the headquarters of the foundation. Cutter, back to himself now, feisty and energetic, would be staying with Mrs. Peters and her son for a few days, although Quinn had the idea he'd better start looking into crates for transporting the dog wherever they were going. He wouldn't mind having the dog along on a lot of operations; he'd more than proved his usefulness.

As had Hayley. When the chips were down, she'd come through beautifully. For the first time he was entertaining the idea that maybe he could have it all. That maybe she was right, that in the past, he'd just never found the right person.

He couldn't be sure it would really work, not until they tried. But try they would. Because he did know, deep in his gut, that if it couldn't work with Hayley, it would never work with anyone.

Well, Hayley and Cutter.

Just the thought of the dog made him smile; it seemed to Quinn that Cutter thought he himself had brought them all together on purpose.

And who knows, maybe he had.

Hayley sat up, shoving her hair back, yawning before saying, "Quinn?"

Her voice never failed to make him smile, just because. He

lay there and just looked at her, letting it flow over him, that sense of peace he'd never found anywhere else.

"What?"

"Who's Charlie?"

He laughed; she'd repeated the question almost daily since they'd been here.

He answered as he always did.

"You'll see."

And she would. Today. The first day of a future that seemed brighter than anything but her smile.

* * * * *

SUSPENSE

COMING NEXT MONTH
AVAILABLE MARCH 27, 2012

REQUEST YOUR FREE BOOKS!
2 FREE NOVELS PLUS 2 FREE GIFTS!

ROMANTIC
SUSPENSE
Sparked by Danger, Fueled by Passion.

YES! Please send me 2 FREE Harlequin® Romantic Suspense novels and my 2 FREE gifts (gifts are worth about $10). After receiving them, if I don't wish to receive any more books, I can return the shipping statement marked "cancel." If I don't cancel, I will receive 4 brand-new novels every month and be billed just $4.49 per book in the U.S. or $5.24 per book in Canada. That's a saving of at least 14% off the cover price! It's quite a bargain! Shipping and handling is just 50¢ per book in the U.S. and 75¢ per book in Canada.* I understand that accepting the 2 free books and gifts places me under no obligation to buy anything. I can always return a shipment and cancel at any time. Even if I never buy another book, the two free books and gifts are mine to keep forever.

240/340 HDN FEFR

Name	(PLEASE PRINT)	
Address		Apt. #
City	State/Prov.	Zip/Postal Code
Signature (if under 18, a parent or guardian must sign)		

Mail to the Reader Service:
IN U.S.A.: P.O. Box 1867, Buffalo, NY 14240-1867
IN CANADA: P.O. Box 609, Fort Erie, Ontario L2A 5X3

Not valid for current subscribers to Harlequin Romantic Suspense books.

Want to try two free books from another line?
Call 1-800-873-8635 or visit www.ReaderService.com.

* Terms and prices subject to change without notice. Prices do not include applicable taxes. Sales tax applicable in N.Y. Canadian residents will be charged applicable taxes. Offer not valid in Quebec. This offer is limited to one order per household. All orders subject to credit approval. Credit or debit balances in a customer's account(s) may be offset by any other outstanding balance owed by or to the customer. Please allow 4 to 6 weeks for delivery. Offer available while quantities last.

Your Privacy—The Reader Service is committed to protecting your privacy. Our Privacy Policy is available online at www.ReaderService.com or upon request from the Reader Service.

We make a portion of our mailing list available to reputable third parties that offer products we believe may interest you. If you prefer that we not exchange your name with third parties, or if you wish to clarify or modify your communication preferences, please visit us at www.ReaderService.com/consumerschoice or write to us at Reader Service Preference Service, P.O. Box 9062, Buffalo, NY 14269. Include your complete name and address.

HRS11B

❖ Harlequin®

ROMANTIC

SUSPENSE

Danger is hot on their heels!

Catch the thrill with author

LINDA CONRAD

Chance, Texas

Sam Chance, a U.S. marshal in the Witness Security
Service, is sworn to protect Grace Brown and her
one-year-old son after Grace testifies against an infamous
drug lord and he swears revenge. With Grace on the edge of
fleeing, Sam knows there is only one safe place he can take
her—home. But when the danger draws near, it's not just
Sam's life on the line but his heart, too.

Watch out for

Texas Baby Sanctuary

Available April 2012

Texas Manhunt

Available May 2012

www.Harlequin.com

Taft Bowman knew he'd ruined any chance he'd had for happiness with Laura Pendleton when he drove her away years ago…and into the arms of another man, thousands of miles away. Now she was back, a widow with two small children…and despite himself, he was starting to believe in second chances.

Harlequin Special® Edition® presents a new installment in USA TODAY *bestselling author* RaeAnne Thayne's *miniseries,* THE COWBOYS OF COLD CREEK.

Enjoy a sneak peek of A COLD CREEK REUNION

Available April 2012 from Harlequin® Special Edition®

A younger woman stood there, and from this distance he had only a strange impression, as though she was somehow standing on an island of calm amid the chaos of the scene, the flashing lights of the emergency vehicles, shouts between his crew members, the excited buzz of the crowd.

And then the woman turned and he just about tripped over a snaking fire hose somebody shouldn't have left there.

Laura.

He froze, and for the first time in fifteen years as a firefighter, he forgot about the incident, his mission, just what the hell he was doing here.

Laura.

Ten years. He hadn't seen her in all that time, since the week before their wedding when she had given him back his ring and left town. Not just town. She had left the whole damn country, as if she couldn't run far enough to get away from him.

Some part of him desperately wanted to think he had made some kind of mistake. It couldn't be her. That was just some other slender woman with a long sweep of honey-blond hair and big, blue, unforgettable eyes. But no. It was definitely Laura. Sweet and lovely.

Not his.

He was going to have to go over there and talk to her. He didn't want to. He wanted to stand there and pretend he hadn't seen her. But he was the fire chief. He couldn't hide out just because he had a painful history with the daughter of the property owner.

Sometimes he hated his job.

Will Taft and Laura be able to make the years recede…or is the gulf between them too broad to ever cross?

Find out in
A COLD CREEK REUNION
Available April 2012 from Harlequin® Special Edition®
wherever books are sold.

Celebrate the 30th anniversary
of Harlequin® Special Edition® with a bonus story
included in each Special Edition® book in April!

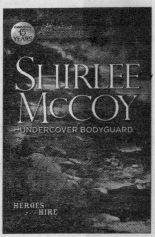